Miracles for the Maharaja

Book III of

Meandering Magicians

Read the first two books of MEANDERING MAGICIANS by Aditi Krishnakumar

The Magicians of Madh
Murder in Melucha

Read more for young adults from Duckbill

The Lies We Tell by Himanjali Sankar
Talking of Muskaan by Himanjali Sankar
Zombiestan by Mainak Dhar
Jobless Clueless Reckless by Revathi Suresh
Facebook Phantom by Suzanne Sangi
The Right Kind of Dog by Adil Jussawalla
Shiva & the Rise of the Shadows by Kanika Dhillon
The Wordkeepers by Jash Sen
Skyserpents by Jash Sen
Daddy Come Lately by Rupa Gulab
Unbroken by Nandhika Nambi
When She Went Away by Andaleeb Wajid
Mirror, Mirror by Andaleeb Wajid
Invisible People by Harsh Mander
When Morning Comes by Arushi Raina
Year of the Weeds by Siddhartha Sarma
Queen of Earth by Devika Rangachari
Queen of Ice by Devika Rangachari
Queen of Fire by Devika Rangachari

Miracles for the Maharaja

Book III of MEANDERING MAGICIANS

ADITI KRISHNAKUMAR

duckbill

An imprint of Penguin Random House

To Divya, who will soon be old enough to read this book for herself—and will, I hope, always believe in magic.

DUCKBILL BOOKS

USA | Canada | UK | Ireland | Australia
New Zealand | India | South Africa | China

Duckbill Books is part of the Penguin Random House group of companies
whose addresses can be found at global.penguinrandomhouse.com

Published by Penguin Random House India Pvt. Ltd
4th Floor, Capital Tower 1, MG Road,
Gurugram 122 002, Haryana, India

Penguin
Random House
India

First published in Duckbill Books by
Penguin Random House India 2023

Text copyright © Aditi Krishnakumar 2023

Aditi Krishnakumar asserts the moral right to be
identified as the author of this work.

ISBN 9780143458074

Typeset in Sitka by DiTech Publishing Services Pvt. Ltd
Printed at Replika Press Pvt. Ltd, India

www.penguin.co.in

The Mortal Realm and the Inter-Realm

The Mortal Realm: The Free Lands

The Free Lands are a part of the Mortal Realm covered by the Inter-Realm Accord. A few of the more prominent are listed below:

THE KINGDOM OF PÜR is the largest of the Free Lands, and the third-largest country in the Mortal Realm. The northern part is ruled from the capital city of Rajgir. The southern part, which is largely autonomous, is ruled from the city of Madh.

Pür is ruled by a Maharaja and a Council of Ministers.

MELUCHA is a prosperous city-state on the banks of the River Nati. Its location provides access to the ocean and major trade routes, which might account for the easy availability of poisons from around the world.

The current ruler of Melucha is the Prince Regnant.

KHAND is a mountainous and thickly forested principality. Very few foreigners have ever been permitted to visit the interior of the country. The tendency of Khand's many rivers to flood means that there is no fixed capital. The ruler and court move around in a constant effort to keep their feet dry.

Khand is ruled by the Moon Princess.

STHAN, which is only slightly smaller in area than Pür (but has a far smaller population) consists of vast swathes of flat land suitable for grazing and agriculture. Sthan is the largest exporter of wheat in the Free Lands; its merchant ships, in fact, are recognized and respected throughout the Mortal Realm.

Sthan is ruled by the Queen, who lives in the walled city of Neeldurg.

SALA is an island nation, the westernmost of the Free Lands. It is known for being the native habitat of a number of critically endangered plants and animals, both magical and non-magical. Traffic between Sala and other countries is strongly discouraged in order to protect its fragile ecosystem. Its capital is Havur.

Sala is ruled by the Lady of the Isle.

VRAJA is a swampy country. What few outsiders know is that, in addition to mangroves and salt marshes, it is home to some of the finest libraries outside Madh, owing to a strong cultural belief that the best way not to get eaten by a crocodile is to be indoors reading a book. Its capital is Magar.

Vraja is ruled by the High Lord.

YAUNA is separated from the rest of the Free Lands by a belt of countries that are not signatories to the Inter-Realm Accord. The chief export of Yauna is philosophy; it provides a steady stream of professors to schools and universities across the Free Lands. The capital of Yauna is Liva.

Yauna is ruled by the Tyrant.

The Inter-Realm

More properly called the Realm between Realms, the Inter-Realm consists mainly of Chaos, interspersed with cities where the various classes of Immortal beings live. Mortals can visit the Inter-Realm, and citizens of the Free Lands are permitted to do so under the Inter-Realm Accord. However, most visitors prefer not to stay very long. Beings from the Inter-Realm can, and frequently do, visit the Mortal Realm, either willingly or as a result of being Summoned by a magician.

Dramatis Personae

In Madh

PARAS, Master Sorcerer and hereditary Governor of the Southern Provinces of the Kingdom of Pür. Paras is the most powerful magician of his generation and more interested in Alchemy than in administration, which he prefers to leave to his brother, to the general relief of everyone who thinks tax disputes shouldn't involve indoor thunderstorms.

ASAMANJAS, Paras's brother, the first child of the family in several generations with no magical ability whatsoever. He doesn't regret this lack, being of the belief that while it's all very well to know how to make it rain out-of-season, it's much more important to know how to placate angry nobles whose best silks have been ruined by unexpected precipitation.

KAMAKSHI, a magician specializing in zoology and exploration. She spends most of her time exploring remote lands, much to the relief of the Arcane Zoology Authorization Desk. Married to Paras.

MEENAKSHI, Paras and Kamakshi's only child and a student at the Royal Academy of Science, Magic and the Arts. A brilliant student but lacking in social skills. Her greatest fear is small talk and the lessons in statecraft that her uncle insists she must take in preparation for her eventual role as Governor.

GOPALI and **SAHA**, Meenakshi's secretaries, responsible for ensuring that such minor duties of state as she is entrusted with are carried out. Both are clever, firm, and have several unusual skills.

NALINI, Head of the Inter-Realm Liaison Bureau, responsible for maintaining good relations between the Kingdom of Pür, particularly the City of Madh, and the Inter-Realm, where all classes of Immortal beings live. Nalini has an ongoing feud with Asamanjas, and constantly encourages him to retire to a remote village for the sake of his health.

THE MASTER OF THE ACADEMY, the Head of the Royal Academy of Science, Magic and the Arts. As students, he and Paras had a rivalry that, far from being outgrown, has deepened over the years into strong mutual dislike. Since the Master of the Academy also favours magical means of dispute resolution, their arguments are hotly anticipated when things in the city are dull.

THE COUNSELLOR, whose profession is described by those sufficiently crass as that of spymaster. He makes a point of knowing everything that's happening in Madh. It is rumoured (though this has never been substantiated) that he once worked as a paid assassin. The Counsellor and his staff work in bright, airy rooms with no secret doors or hidden passages.

CLEVER RAMAN, one of the most dedicated students the Royal Academy of Science, Magic and the Arts has ever known. He is called Clever Raman to distinguish him from his classmate, Tall Raman. It is Clever Raman's avowed ambition to be Master of the Academy as soon as he can; that has caused the present Master of the Academy to mysteriously lose all his applications for a month's fieldwork in Melucha.

In Melucha

SHEL, the Prince Regnant. Often considered by outsiders a purely ornamental feature of the landscape, Shel is in reality a shrewd and astute ruler. Would be handsome if not for his insistence on cultivating a goatee.

PERSIS, the Princess Consort. Once a young and powerful sorceress of surpassing beauty known for turning trespassers into pigs, Persis has since learnt to control her impulses. She is now an older, powerful sorceress of beauty undiminished—and she is far more frightening.

KALBAN, the elder of Shel and Persis's two sons and Prince-Heir of Melucha (though in Melucha nobody can be certain of the throne until they're sitting on it—and usually not even then). Kalban inherited his mother's magical ability, which doesn't endear him to the people of his homeland. Spent the past several years as a member of Paras's household in Madh, studying at the Royal Academy of Science, Magic and the Arts.

ABHINAV, the younger of Shel and Persis's sons. Abhinav has no magical gifts at all, and has taken advantage of the years of Kalban's absence to make himself the more popular choice to succeed his father as Prince Regnant.

RATI, a noblewoman of Melucha. Although the youngest of several children, it somehow came about that Rati inherited her parents' estate. Consequently, she is sympathetic to those who consider primogeniture a suboptimal way of deciding matters of inheritance.

DEV, an artist and sculptor married to Rati. It is said by some people that Dev owes his professional success to his wife's wealth and position. These are, naturally, jealous, small-minded individuals who have no appreciation for high art.

In Rajgir

THE MAHARAJA, who was, at birth, behind thirty-seven aunts, uncles and cousins for the throne of Pür. After taking what he considered his destined place, he settled into a life of placid inaction, interspersed by occasional spells of eliminating all threats to his position.

THE MAHARANI, who would never have married somebody thirty-eighth in line to the throne if she hadn't noticed a can-do spirit about him. The Maharani likes to focus on her traditional role of maintaining good relations with the rulers of other countries, though sometimes the rulers of other countries try her patience.

VASUNDHARA, only grandchild of the Maharaja and Maharani, she followed tradition by joining the army as a teenager and rising through the ranks by dint of hard work, dedication, and the ability to shout insults at the enemy across the cacophony of a battlefield. Her lack of interest in choosing a consort has been a matter of worry to her grandparents.

In the Inter-Realm

RAMBHA, one of the chief Celestial Dancers. Rambha has seen great magicians turn to darkness and empires rise and fall, and she has very little faith in mortals.

CHITRALEKHA first met Meenakshi and Kalban in Madh, when they found themselves on the same side of an investigation into a series of mysterious incidents. Chitralekha *wants* to like them, but she has a Celestial Dancer's instinctive suspicion of any mortal magician. After all, if mortal magicians didn't have a tendency to cause devastation, there wouldn't be any need for Celestial Dancers.

PROLOGUE

'What do you think?'

The Maharaja of Pür held up two swatches of brocade, one red and silver and the other green and gold, and looked inquiringly at his wife, who was sitting at her desk answering letters.

The Maharani of Pür cast the swatches a look of disinterest and went on with her correspondence.

'Well?' the Maharaja pressed. 'Which should I have?'

'If you ask me,' said the Maharani, signing her name with a vindictive pressure that nearly tore the paper and boded ill for the recipient of the letter, 'neither.'

'We *should* match, shouldn't we? It'll look better in the portraits.' The Maharaja put down the swatches and poured himself a cup of wine. 'What are *you* wearing? Your dressmaker wouldn't tell me.'

'She *couldn't* tell you,' corrected the Maharani. 'I haven't decided. What does it matter about the portraits? You can tell the royal artist you have a fancy for being depicted as a gandharva in a flying chariot and he'll do it.'

The Maharani pulled the next letter from her stack. It dispelled her ill humour at once. She went so far as to smile.

The Maharaja knew that smile. In the days of their courtship, when he'd been young, foolish and at the very back of the line to be ruler of Pür, he'd called it charming. Now he *knew* it was dangerous. He only hoped it wasn't dangerous for *him*.

'Kamakshi's written to say she can come,' said the Maharani.

Fortunately, the cup the Maharaja was holding was a simple, everyday affair, not made of fine crystal or encrusted with gemstones. When it slipped from his nerveless fingers, the only damage it sustained was a small dent that the palace goldsmith would repair overnight.

The Maharani clicked her tongue and lifted her sari out of the way of the spreading puddle of wine.

'Kamakshi is coming?' the Maharaja said, in a tone that indicated that Kamakshi was the leader of a leap of hungry leopards. '*Kamakshi?*'

'Yes.'

'I thought she was in the Eastern Isles!'

'She was. She *is* at the moment. But her daughter is taking her magical licence Tests and, naturally, Kamakshi wants to be in Madh to provide moral support to Meenakshi—'

'Gods have mercy,' said the Maharaja, who had dreamed of being an actor in his youth and still liked to extract all the drama he could from every situation. Finding his hands empty, he poured himself another cup of wine and quaffed it. 'Paras and Kamakshi's daughter in the capital and licensed to practice magic in public.'

'No, that's *one* mercy. The Tests are after the swayamvara.'

'Did you arrange it that way?'

'What an idea! Testing future magicians is a vitally important process. If I were to interfere with it, I would be in violation of the International Code of Sorcery, the Inter-Realm Accord, and any number of paragraphs and by-laws of the constitution of the Royal Academy. It would be anarchy.'

'Oh.' The Maharaja shrugged. Not being a magician himself, he had little interest in the International Code of Sorcery. 'Just as well. Melucha and Vraja are attending the swayamvara. They don't like magic.'

'Melucha won't be a problem. Persis and the Prince Regnant know Paras and Kamakshi, and Kalban spent several years in Madh. I believe Meenakshi was in Melucha last year to learn statecraft—if something doesn't bode well for us, it's *that*. Vraja, I agree, requires caution. Still, they know the realities of the world. I'm sure it'll be fine. Speaking of guests, have you heard back from the Yaunic Ambassador?'

'The Tyrant-in-waiting sent his regrets. The duties of heir apparent do not allow him to attend. The Ambassador will be most delighted to be present at all events.' The Maharaja sighed. 'As a way of distracting Vasundhara from that unsuitable youth, this plan isn't an unqualified success.'

'We have *weeks*. Something will work out.'

'How? Most of them are far too young, and those who aren't ... '

'Vraja's sister's children *are* the right age. And they're not in line to inherit, so I'm sure one of them will be happy to come and live here. Better to be consort to the future Maharani of Pür than to be an inconvenient cousin in that crocodile-infested swamp.'

'Vraja's sister's children are boring.'

'That defeatist attitude isn't helping. What's the worst that could happen?'

'The *worst* is that Vasundhara will reject all the eligible suitors, and insist on marrying that complete *outsider—*'

'Would that be so bad? I can see why she likes him— he's handsome—'

'Yes, but—'

'Rich, not that *that's* a concern—'

'Yes, but—'

'Has an *excellent* seat on a horse, which is what one looks for in a royal consort—'

'Yes, but he's a *Sprite.*'

When their granddaughter Vasundhara had announced her engagement to the family, the Maharaja's first reaction had been relief. The first duty of the heir to the throne was to produce the *next* heir to the throne, and until then he had been in some doubt as to whether his granddaughter would perform that duty. She had gone twenty-five years without showing interest in anything other than military training.

Then her betrothed had come round to dinner. The discovery that he was a Sprite had caused general consternation. To add to the Maharaja's dismay, instead of being accompanied, as was traditional, by his immediate family, he had come alone. He had, however, been followed the next day by a furious missive from the Inter-Realm Ambassador demanding to know *what* the Maharaja of Pür had been thinking to condone this insanity.

'Being a Sprite isn't so bad,' said the Maharani. 'People used to marry Sprites and Celestial Dancers all the time.'

'People. Not the only heir to the throne of Pür. You *know* it's different.'

'I know,' said the Maharani, a pensive look coming into her eyes. She had been fond of their only child, Vasundhara's father.

'If she'd had a sister or brother,' the Maharaja went on, 'it wouldn't matter so much.'

'I daresay. But she doesn't. She'll make an excellent queen. There's no need to worry about that.'

'That's not what I'm worried about.' The Maharaja picked up his swatches of brocade again. 'Maybe I'll just ask for gold-on-gold. Gold goes with everything.'

'Just as you like,' said the Maharani, slitting open another envelope. She wrinkled her nose. 'Oh no. How infuriating!'

'What is it?'

The Maharani got to her feet and went to the door. Her tread was brisk. She opened the door and beckoned to someone outside. 'Find Princess Vasundhara and tell her the Maharaja wants to see her at once.'

'What is it?' asked the Maharaja again. When he was told that he wanted to see his granddaughter at once, what followed was seldom a soothing chat. 'What did Vasundhara do?'

'The Inter-Realm Ambassador is threatening to boycott the swayamvara because we didn't obtain his approval before allowing Ravi to enter the lists.'

'Not *he*,' said the Maharaja with feeling. 'He hasn't missed any of our feasts yet.'

'He *is* fond of them,' agreed the Maharani, smiling. 'It's been useful. Don't you remember the trouble we had with the Dancer they sent before him? She couldn't stomach mortal foods and she sat and scowled through every important event. This is better. He'll come, but we'll have to make an apology in the proper form. Vasundhara's caused this trouble. She might as well deal with it.'

CHAPTER I

'Step through! *Step through!*'

The woman who stepped through the portal had never been bawled at so robustly in her life. She opened her mouth to protest the treatment and then stopped when she saw the size of the crowd in the Portals Hall.

'Is *everyone* in the Free Lands here?' asked her companion.

'Only half of them.' She followed an impatiently beckoning hand in the direction of a door bearing the legend 'Diplomatic Visitors'. 'I suppose the Princess of Pür choosing a husband attracts the hopeful.'

'Or the hope*less*,' said her companion with a sniff.

'Perhaps you might save your witticisms until we're at the Embassy?'

'I don't see why we can't have a portal in the Embassy,' her companion grumbled. 'It would save us all this mingling . . . Or at least, we could have come last week when the Prince's family did.'

The woman handed a form to the official at the desk. Because this was the Diplomatic Visitors desk, the official contrived to look only a little bored as he scanned the document.

'Rati, from Melucha? And this is . . . Dev? Anything to declare?'

'No.'

'Poisons, knives, other weapons?'

'How uncouth.'

The official shrugged. 'Normally, we don't bother diplomatic visitors, but after the incident yesterday, we've increased security. Any luggage?'

'Sent ahead. What incident yesterday?'

'You'll hear about it at your embassy. Go through, please.'

Trailed by Dev, Rati made her way outside. A carriage with the crest of Melucha emblazoned on the door was waiting in the portico. Rati greeted the unfamiliar driver and got in.

They drove in silence along busy streets for several minutes. Elaborate gardens were on either side. Rati could name only a handful of the flowers that scented the air. She had had a thorough education in botany, by the standards of Melucha, which meant she could identify every poisonous plant by root, stem and leaf, but her knowledge of decorative blooms was limited.

'Does this city never end?' Dev muttered.

'We're taking the long way around,' Rati replied. 'To avoid cutting through the centre of the city. We might spend hours stuck in the crowd there. We'll be at the Embassy soon.'

It was another half hour before the carriage finally drew to a halt in the courtyard of the Embassy of Melucha. A large sign outside informed all comers that they were now on Meluchan soil and unlicensed magic was banned.

'It happens all the time, though,' Rati warned Dev. 'The Maharaja has a lax attitude to the regulation of magic, so nobody takes the warning seriously.'

'Why are we even here? Neither of us is participating in the swayamvara.'

'We are here because nearly everyone of any importance in all the Free Lands is here. Try to make some friends.'

⚜

In the back garden of the Embassy of Melucha, quite as beautiful as any of the other gardens of the city, but far more dangerous to the idle taker of walks and nibbler of berries, two young men were arguing over a plant.

'That can't *possibly* be the one he meant, Kalban,' said the younger of the two. 'He said the *fourth* from the end—'

'He said deadly nightshade! The fourth from the end is *woody* nightshade.'

'Look, let's just take both.'

'And get a lecture about not paying attention? No, thank you. We're taking the deadly nightshade.'

'Why are we doing this, anyway? Can't the Embassy staff help?'

'They *grow* the plants. That's all you can expect. You can't ask the staff to help you brew poisons outside Melucha. They don't have diplomatic immunity. They'll be arrested as co-conspirators if we murder someone.'

'It's a demonstration—and only because the Yaunic Ambassador specifically asked for one. We should take both plants. We can tell Father we thought he could use the other one to compare— what's *that*?'

That was a building just visible across the lengths of three intervening gardens. The windows of one wing had begun flashing with light.

'Madh!' Kalban leapt to his feet. 'Meenakshi said they were going to open portals directly into the High Commission instead of coming through the Portals Hall.'

'Mother said that would take far too much paperwork.'

'Yes, because Melucha is another country. Madh is part of Pür. The only paperwork is what the Portals Regulation Authority wants.' He glanced down at the two plants. 'What should we do about this?'

'Never mind, I'll deal with the supplies for the demonstration,' said Abhinav. 'You can go and greet your friends.'

'So that you can show Father how dedicated you are, while I'm off having a good time?'

'Maybe.' Abhinav shrugged. 'So what? You do realize nobody thinks you're good at botany, don't you? The one thing you have in your favour is that you get on with the Master Sorcerer. You might as well go. I'm sure Mother will come join you as soon as she's dealt with Rati.'

Kalban hesitated a moment longer. Then he went down the garden path to the back gate.

'Keep it moving,' snapped the official from the Portals Regulation Authority. 'Don't dawdle. You should all have received your room allocations before leaving Madh. Please remember that only licensed practitioners may perform magic outside the High Commission grounds.'

'She didn't have to look right *at* me when she said that,' muttered the young woman exiting the portal with two companions.

'You didn't have to sneak your griffon to Rajgir under an Illusion, Meenakshi, but here we are.'

'You *know* about the griffon?'

'Could Saha and I have failed to notice the large gap you left between us and the junior deputies from the Inter-Realm Liaison Bureau?'

'He won't get in anyone's way. He would have been bored by himself in Madh . . . and it's going to be more boring than usual here. Royal events always are. This was an inconvenient time to have the swayamvara. The new Alchemy lab at the Academy has just opened. It's got stable rooms for the creation of magical objects. I've barely had a chance to use them. Mother wouldn't even let me bring my books.'

'With good reason. Nobody wants to be dealing with the aftermath of a flock of chimeras running loose in the middle of a wedding.' They stopped at the door, where a man was ticking names off on a list. 'I'm Gopali, this is Saha, that's Meenakshi.'

'Oh, good. The Master Sorcerer's been asking for her. You were expected earlier this morning.' He handed Meenakshi a sheet of paper. 'Mortal Realm portals regulations are being relaxed for the duration of the swayamvara. Details are there.'

'We were delayed,' said Gopali. 'She'll go and see the Master Sorcerer at once. Do you know where he is?'

'He's meeting some people in the morning room.'

'Not Vraja, is it? Then it's all right. Meenakshi, go and see what your father wants . . . Wait!' Gopali pulled her away from the door. 'Leave the griffon in your room. We'll deal with it.'

The three of them hurried upstairs. A few minutes later, Meenakshi came back down.

The morning room was a small, sunny room, meant to hold half a dozen people at most. When Meenakshi went in, it seemed as though a quarter of the city's population must be crammed into it. Her parents and uncle were there, along with the Maharaja and Maharani of Pür, Princess Vasundhara, a handful of royal guards, Princess Persis of Melucha, Kalban (who, looking distinctly uncomfortable in his Meluchan silks, waved at her from the windowsill to which he had been relegated), two men Meenakshi didn't know but who from their clothes and turbans must be ministers, and Nalini, the Head of the Inter-Realm Liaison Bureau.

'What happened?' Meenakshi asked warily. 'Whatever it is, I didn't do it. I arrived ten minutes ago. I've had no time to do anything.'

'Meenakshi,' Nalini said, 'I don't believe you've met Bahuka, Pür's Minister for Inter-Realm Affairs. He's the Maharaja's cousin.'

One of the men gave her a brief, awkward nod. Meenakshi studied him covertly. She knew, because Kalban had told her, that being the Maharaja's cousin was dangerous to one's health. Bahuka must be very competent if he had not only survived, but risen to a high position.

'Tejas is the Minister for Law and Order.'

The other man didn't acknowledge the introduction at all.

'We have a problem,' said the Maharani. 'A friend of Vasundhara's—'

'My *betrothed*,' corrected the Princess.

'There is no betrothal until the swayamvara is complete,' said the Maharani firmly. 'You're in the direct line of succession. That's the law. Vasundhara's *friend* has disappeared.'

'The Sprite?'

'Does *everyone* know she wants to marry a Sprite?' muttered the Maharaja.

'We were going to do everything properly,' said Vasundhara. 'He was planning to come to Rajgir for the swayamvara.'

'I thought he was here already, working for the Inter-Realm Embassy. Isn't that how you met him?'

'After we announced our intentions two months ago, he was recalled. Then Grandmother had a letter from the Ambassador saying that he'd disappeared from the Inter-Realm and wanting to know if we had any idea where he might be.'

'How long has he been missing?'

'He came to Rajgir a month ago to prepare for the swayamvara because he knew he'd have to win honestly, no magic—I didn't know he'd come back until last week. He came to the palace to add his name to the list. I saw him then.'

'If you saw him, how is he missing?'

'He's disappeared from Rajgir.' Vasundhara turned to the ministers. 'Just give her the letter. That's easier than trying to explain.'

The Minister for Inter-Realm Affairs gave Meenakshi a scrap of paper. Meenakshi unfolded it.

If you want to see the Sprite again, bring me the Fire of the East. You have one week. You will receive further instructions.

'It came last night with a ring I had given Ravi,' Vasundhara said. 'Whoever wrote that letter—either they have him, or they got the ring from him somehow. They must know where he is.'

Meenakshi looked up. 'The Fire of the East? That's just a legend.'

'That's what we all thought. Apparently, it isn't,' Nalini said. 'I spoke to the Inter-Realm Ambassador this morning. He didn't want to admit it, but given the circumstances . . . ' She glanced at Meenakshi's mother. 'Perhaps you'd better tell this part. It's not my area of expertise.'

'The Fire of the East,' said Kamakshi, 'is a large fire agate. It was discovered a very long time ago—I don't know exactly how long, but at least seven hundred years—and is believed to have been formed when a magical attack, part of an Inter-Realm battle, led to a volcanic eruption in the Eastern Isles. The legend says it has its own magic. According to the Inter-Realm Ambassador, that isn't true. It only acts as a focus to amplify the user's own magic. Considerably.'

'And as such,' said her brother-in-law, Asamanjas, 'it is a Class V Forbidden Magical Artefact under the terms of the Inter-Realm Accord. If we try to find it, leave alone hand it over to some criminal, Pür will be in violation of the Accord. I *cannot* stress this enough.'

'I take it that means we're going to try to find it?' Meenakshi asked, smiling at her uncle's disgruntlement. Now things were looking up.

'Not *we*,' said Nalini. 'You heard your uncle. *We* can't violate the Inter-Realm Accord.'

'If there's a Sprite missing—'

'Have you learnt nothing of Inter-Realm bureaucracy? The Sprites are concerned about their missing friend. We are doing everything we can to find him. There'll be investigators from the Inter-Realm collaborating with the Rajgir City Guard. But Class V Forbidden Magical Artefacts are given that label for a reason. Rambha doesn't want to risk someone finding it and . . . you know what might happen if it's knocking around in the Mortal Realm.'

'What we hope, my dear,' said the Maharani, 'is that *you* will consent to look for it.' She glanced around the room. 'I can speak freely in this company. You're underage *and* you're not yet Licensed, so anything you do isn't a violation of the Accord. There would be some minor consequences. I expect the Magical Activities Legislative Board would send you some literature on the subject of the Inter-Realm Accord. What's a pamphlet or two in such an important cause?'

'Of course,' said Meenakshi's father, Paras, 'we're all completely ready to help.'

'Some of us more than others,' said Asamanjas, glaring at his brother.

'I can do more than help,' volunteered Vasundhara. 'I'm not a magician. The Accord doesn't apply to me.'

'I'd rather not put that to the test,' said Nalini. 'It might be argued that the future ruler of Pür is covered by the Accord, whether she can do magic or not. The point is, Meenakshi, if the missing Sprite were to be damaged by whoever has taken him, the consequences would be disastrous. We can't risk it during a major state event. While nobody believes in the Inter-Realm Accord, letter and spirit, more strongly than I do—'

'What Nalini is trying to say,' interrupted Kamakshi, 'is that although there will be trouble if we look for the Fire of the East, that's nothing on the trouble there will be if a Sprite is harmed by a human magician. If worse comes to worst, we need to have the gem, at least to give us some leverage over the kidnapper.'

'Don't worry about Vasundhara,' put in the Maharani. 'She may want to gallivant all over Rajgir on a quest and I'm sure she's only regretting that there are no dragons to slay, but she won't have time. The swayamvara begins the day after tomorrow.'

'We're not still having it!' Vasaundhara protested.

'Yes, we are,' the Maharani said implacably. 'You don't stop a swayamvara just because one guest doesn't turn up. At your great-aunt's swayamvara there were three duels to the death. She didn't let that prevent her from getting on with things.'

'Perhaps you can take up this debate later,' Nalini said. 'Your mother and Persis and I,' she went on to Meenakshi, 'are going to work with the City Guard and track down the kidnapper. Will you look for the gem? You'll have to keep your activities secret from anybody who is not in this room right now.'

Meenakshi smiled.

CHAPTER II

'We need a plan of action.' Every bedroom in the High Commission of Madh came with an attached study suitable for Summoning or other forms of magic. Meenakshi led the way into hers. 'What do we know about the Fire of the East?'

Vasundhara, who had accompanied Kalban and Meenakshi upstairs, said, 'Your mother told us about it before you came. There have been no sightings, confirmed or unconfirmed, of the Fire of the East since before the Inter-Realm Accord was signed. The last person who claimed to have it was Tara the Starchaser, rival of the Great Sorceress Anasuya.'

'Tara the Starchaser?' asked Meenakshi. 'The foremother of Pür, whose great-grandson signed the Inter-Realm Accord?'

'Tara the Starchaser, whose great-grandson founded Rajgir,' added Kalban. 'So there's a possibility that the gem is here, if she really had it and passed it on to her descendants. We should go to the library to look at the city's records.'

'If it were that simple, there'd be no need for anyone to kidnap a Sprite,' said Meenakshi. 'The library's open to everyone. Are there any old stories or songs that might refer to the Fire of the East?'

'I don't spend time listening to court bards,' Vasundhara said. 'But if you come to the palace, I can introduce you to my cousin Rajesh. He's by way of being a historian. He's useful and his dearest ambition is to be a scribe. I'm planning to keep him around.'

'Library it is,' Meenakshi said brightly. 'Are you allowed to come and help me?' she asked Kalban. 'Or will they disown you in Melucha?'

Kalban shrugged. 'What does it matter? Melucha needn't worry about what's happening across half a continent. I'll come to the library with you. What about you?' he added to Vasundhara.

'Long hours poring over musty books? No, thank you. I deal in the *real* world. Call me if you need someone to face down ferocious beasts guarding the path to the gem. Meanwhile, I don't like it, but my grandmother's right. I need to go make sure everything's set up for the beginning of the swayamvara. The first test is archery.'

'I pity the people who have to take any archery test she sets up,' said Kalban with a shudder, when Vasundhara had left. 'Fortunately, it isn't me. Library now?'

'Yes, I suppose we'd better. There's something you should know first.'

'What?' Kalban asked warily. In the past, *there's something you should know first* had been the presage of the secretary of the Arcane Zoology Authorization Desk coming to him with a litany of complaints.

'I brought the griffon with me.'

'Of course you did. I suppose it's too much to hope that you filled in the necessary forms to bring a dangerous alchemical beast into Rajgir?'

'He's *gentle*. And he's not *in* Rajgir. The High Commission of Madh is the territory of Madh. *You* told me that.'

'*That* you remember?'

'It's just as well I brought him. Griffons have a natural affinity for treasure. He can help us find it.'

'Does anyone else know he's here?'

'Only Gopali and Saha.'

Kalban nodded. Gopali and Saha, as anyone who worked with Meenakshi must be, were level-headed, inured to shocks, and, above all, *discreet*.

'Let's go to the library.'

Saha, Meenakshi's junior secretary, stopped them in the corridor.

'Just where are you going?' she demanded. 'We have work to do. There's a state dinner tonight. I need to brief you on the attendees.'

'We're only going to the library. I'll be back in time to get ready for the dinner.'

'We won't be long,' Kalban added.

Then he wished he hadn't spoken, because Saha turned to glare at him. '*You*. You're going with her. You're responsible for making sure she's back here one hour before the dinner begins.'

The Royal Library was a sprawling four-storey building, the lower two levels of which were devoted to public reading rooms. A helpful clerk directed Meenakshi and Kalban to a tiny room in the basement. Its walls were crammed with shelves. Books, scrolls and codices filled every available space.

'All the records of the city,' she said. 'The older ones are at the back.'

Without a word, Meenakshi and Kalban went to the shelf furthest from the door, selected a book each, and took them to the table in the centre of the room.

'This is hopeless,' Kalban said, two hours later. 'I can tell you how many statues of Tara the Starchaser there are in Rajgir—far too many, by the way—but there's nothing about the gem. I have, on the other hand, read some *fascinating* letters by a pretender called Lilavati.'

'It says here that Tara collected many artefacts with purported magical properties.' Meenakshi held up the book she was reading. 'She seems to have had a fondness for . . . knick-knacks. The Enchanted Necklace of the Serpent Queen, the White Jewels of the Sunrise—there's a list. It's long.'

'She wouldn't have been the only one to like pretty things with magical potential. Any idea where any of it is?'

'It says Amsuman—that's her great-grandson—sold most of his inheritance for money to the build the city. It's rumoured that he kept a few pieces, the greatest treasures, for himself. Nobody knows where those items are. Amsuman's son dug up all the gardens and roads trying to find them. He just ended up having to spend a monumental amount on repairing and repaving. Even the most inveterate treasure-hunters don't bother trying to find Amsuman's treasure now. It's regarded as a story propagated by Amsuman himself to make people think he had more than he did.'

'How helpful.' Kalban sighed and got to his feet. 'Come on. We're already going to miss Saha's deadline. If we stay here any longer, I won't have to worry about attending the dinner because she would have killed me.'

'Can we borrow some of these? I can read them at night after the dinner and see if there's anything helpful.'

'I don't see why not. Let's go find that clerk.'

⚕

Fortunately for all concerned, the head of the royal household, who had some experience of Meenakshi, had contrived to place her between Kalban and Nalini at the dinner table. Meenakshi didn't particularly *like* Nalini, but at least she didn't have to make small talk with her.

A young man from Vraja, who intended to participate in the swayamvara and best all other contenders, was seated opposite. This might have been a cause for consternation, but the young man was full of his own prospects and held forth at length, requiring no contribution to the conversation from anybody else.

'Tomorrow is the last day for people to enter the lists,' he said to the lady on one side of him. 'There are already over forty entrants,' he informed the gentleman on the other. 'I am a fine archer,' he added to Meenakshi. 'I expect to do well in the first competition.'

'Ah,' said Meenakshi, knowing that either Nalini or Kalban would pick up the conversation.

Nalini did. While she engaged the young man on the subject of what competitions were expected, Meenakshi looked around the room. Her father was seated by the Maharani, partly because the Master Sorcerer took precedence over everyone else, but mainly so that the Maharani could run interference if he looked like he was about to say anything unfortunate. Her mother was deep in conversation with the High Lord of Vraja.

Rati, four tables over and seemingly participating in a dozen different conversations at once, saw Meenakshi and waved.

'Where's Abhinav?' she whispered to Kalban. 'Didn't he come?'

'He's over there, exchanging notes with the Yaunic Ambassador.'

'The Yaunic Ambassador,' said the youth from Vraja, hearing the end of Kalban's sentence, 'is a good friend of mine. Just yesterday he told me that he thought I was the best candidate for the hand of Princess Vasundhara, and by extension the fittest future royal consort. The Tyrant-in-waiting himself hopes that . . . '

Meenakshi stopped listening.

'Luckily for me,' Kalban said, 'there's nobody suitable from Melucha.'

'No entrants at all?'

'Oh, no, there are two—from lateral branches of minor noble families. They won't last beyond a day or so and I believe they only entered the list because Father specifically asked them to—Melucha has to have *some* entrants,' he said in response to Meenakshi's uncomprehending look. 'It would be a snub to Princess Vasundhara if we didn't. And since Abhinav and I aren't old enough, and naturally, we didn't want to encourage someone who was likely to actually *win* . . . '

'Melucha has to enter someone, but you're hoping they'll lose?'

'Exactly.'

'Why?'

'Because anyone who marries the future Maharani of Pür will be in an excellent position to oust my father from the throne.'

'Kalban,' Nalini said under her breath, 'I know I should be grateful that Meenakshi hasn't tried to relieve her boredom in any creative ways, but if *you* don't help me handle this pompous idiot, I'll know what to do about it.'

꫰

Meenakshi expected to return to her room to find it quiet. Gopali and Saha had left as soon as the dinner was over, claiming to be too tired to stay longer. Meenakshi had been compelled to watch the after-dinner entertainment. The hours of music, dancing, and amateur theatricals had stretched her endurance to the utmost. She was looking forward to reading in silent solitude.

That wasn't to be. Gopali and Saha, far from having gone to bed, were sitting in her room in chairs drawn up on either side of the window. Neither of them looked at all tired. Their upright attitudes radiated disapproval and the readiness to act on it.

Meenakshi was nonplussed. She had returned from the library only a little later than promised. She had attended the dinner, which had proven every bit as tedious as she had expected. She had even remembered to wish the youth from Vraja good luck for the competition. She couldn't think of anything she'd done to merit the lecture that was obviously coming.

For a moment she wondered if the griffon had frightened someone or otherwise misbehaved, but then she saw him curled up in a corner with his head under one wing.

'What?' she asked, shutting the door. 'I've done everything you wanted today.'

'*These.*' Gopali held up the books Meenakshi had brought back. 'Where did you get them?'

'From the Royal Library. It's all right. I signed them out.'

'Why do you even *need* these books?'

'For a little light reading. They're *books*. What's wrong?'

'The entire trunk full of books we brought from Madh isn't enough? The latest edition of *Alchemy* magazine? The Theory of Magic texts you're supposed to be revising before your Tests? You've read them all in less than a day? What do you want with *these*?'

Meenakshi looked at Saha for help.

Saha's face was implacable. 'I can't imagine why you'd be interested in the founding of Rajgir, unless it's for the legend of Amsuman's treasure.'

'You *know* about that?'

'Our job is to keep you out of trouble. We make it a point to be aware of obscure magical legends as insurance against the day when you might decide to take an interest in them . . . as apparently you have now done in this one. The griffons were fine—the Alchemy is fine—*experiments* are fine—but *this*? Nearly every item of Amsuman's alleged treasure is a Class V Forbidden Magical Artefact. The Dark Stone, the Cursed Necklace of the Serpent Queen—'

'*Enchanted* Necklace,' Meenakshi corrected.

'That's what the book says. It's *cursed*. Your rule-breaking is usually harmless, but *this* is too great a risk for you to take.'

'Most of those things probably aren't even real,' Meenakshi pointed out.

'What if they *are* real? What are you going to do if you find one of them?'

'Meenakshi,' Gopali said quietly, 'you'd better tell us what's going on.'

'I suppose I ought,' Meenakshi agreed, sitting on the bed. 'You're bound to find out sooner or later. You know Vasundhara wants to marry a Sprite?'

'Is there anyone in the entire kingdom of Pür who *hasn't* heard of Princess Vasundhara's intentions?'

'He's been kidnapped.'

'Kidnapped? When?'

'I don't know. I suppose they've kept it quiet to avoid causing a disruption to the swayamvara. Vasundhara got a note this morning, demanding the Fire of the East in exchange for Ravi.'

'The Fire of the East? The gem that's rumoured to amplify even a minor magician's power to potentially world-ending levels?'

'The note gave her a week to find it.'

'Well,' Gopali said grudgingly, 'at least you've not *entirely* lost your mind, though I question the wisdom of going and looking for the thing in response to a ransom demand. Does the Head of the Inter-Realm Liaison Bureau know about this?'

'She was the one who asked me to look for it.'

'What?' Saha said, furious. 'I'm going to have a word with her in the morning.'

'She said—'

'I don't *care* what she said! Contravening the Inter-Realm Accord is bad enough. She should, at least, have the nerve to do it herself instead of asking *you* to do it for her.'

'No, I can see why she did that,' said Gopali. 'Meenakshi's not yet licensed. Pür wouldn't be in breach of the Accord, technically . . . But that implies that Nalini's not told Urvashi or Rambha what she's doing.'

She looked at Meenakshi for confirmation. Meenakshi nodded.

'Why wouldn't Nalini tell them?' said Saha. 'This would be an exigent circumstance.'

'Not exigent enough to overrule the Inter-Realm Accord,' said Gopali, 'and Nalini knows it. Class V Forbidden Magical Artefacts are—'

'Forbidden for a reason,' Meenakshi finished. 'Yes, I know. Whoever kidnapped the Sprite, if they . . . '

'What if they kill him when their demands aren't met?' said Gopali. 'I would say it's worth it, wouldn't you?' Meenakshi stared at her. 'I mean it. Ravi's a *Sprite*. Hundreds of years older than the princess. Bad enough that he was foolish and got into a love affair with a mortal woman. To allow himself to be *kidnapped* in the Mortal Realm—'

'He was here for the swayamvara—'

'He made himself vulnerable! Sprites and Dancers aren't supposed to get involved with mortals precisely to prevent things like this from happening. Meenakshi, *think*. Whoever did this timed it well. Ravi's been living in Rajgir for years. He's not been kidnapped in all this time. Why now? The Maharaja's invited everyone in the Free Lands to the swayamvara. Magicians from around the world are here in force—and *you* came today, a powerful magician who has not yet been given her Licence. How fortuitous.'

'You can't be the only one who realized that,' Saha said.

Gopali scoffed. 'The Master Sorcerer may not have thought about it any more than Meenakshi, but I'm sure everyone else has realized how extraordinary the timing is. I'll eat my scarf if Nalini hasn't.'

'Maybe she has,' Meenakshi said, 'but what other option is there?'

'Rambha and Urvashi must be taking *some* action.'

'They're investigating—and Mother and Nalini and Persis. Nalini thinks if they can't find the Sprite and he's harmed . . . it'll mean trouble with the Inter-Realm if it's a mortal who's done it.'

Gopali and Saha looked at each other. 'I suppose it will,' Gopali said slowly. 'The Sprites have been spoiling for a fight ever since Mada was disgraced last year. All they need is an excuse. But giving the Fire of the East to a kidnapper who might do *anything* with it isn't the way to avoid trouble.'

'Nalini's going to interrogate—I forget his name, but the Sprite was staying with him. They're trying to track him down. She says she'll use the Fire of the East only as a bargaining chip, and only if she must.'

'What about you?' Gopali said. 'If you find the Fire of the East, if it's really as powerful as it's believed to be, are you going to give it to someone unscrupulous enough to kidnap a Sprite and demand ransom?'

'I . . . I haven't thought about that,' Meenakshi admitted.

'Do it now.' Gopali stood, taking the books. 'No reading these under the covers. I agree that the circumstances require creative thinking, but that's not the same as *no* thinking. You can have the books back in the morning, if you can convince me that you know what you're doing.'

'I'm doing what the Head of the Inter-Realm Liaison Bureau asked me to do! And *everyone* was there when she did—the Maharaja and Maharani, my parents, my uncle—'

'You can have them back in the morning,' Gopali repeated, 'if you can convince me that *you* know what you're doing.'

CHAPTER III

'You look cheerful,' Abhinav commented, when he and Kalban met in the garden after breakfast. 'Although you're dressed like a peasant. Enjoy yourself at dinner yesterday?'

Kalban shrugged, unperturbed by Abhinav's jibe. It was a beautiful morning, sunshine pouring down so that the grass seemed to sparkle. The weather might make for an unpleasantly warm afternoon, which was why he had eschewed formal clothing in favour of something light and loose. But even the thought of poking about the windowless library basement on a hot day couldn't dampen his spirits. The thought of being able to do as he pleased, a Licensed Magician in Pür, without worrying about the impression it would make on the Privy Council in Melucha, was too uplifting.

'Not really,' he said in response to Abhinav's question. 'I had to listen to one of Vraja's contenders going on and on about his own superior prospects. Luckily, Meenakshi wasn't in much of a mood to talk or she might have told him what *she* thought of his chances of winning the hand of the princess.'

'They're not good, I take it.'

'Vasundhara doesn't *want* to marry anyone other than Ravi, and they're not going to persuade her into it by showing off their skill at archery.'

'Dinner was a washout, then. Why are you still happy?'

'What makes you think I am? Do you know if there's anything important happening this morning?'

'Not unless the Yaunic Ambassador shows up wanting that demonstration of poisons he forgot about yesterday. I hear he's by way of calling himself a magician, though he isn't powerful enough to worry the Tyrant. But don't disappear yet. Rati was asking for you. She wants you to introduce her to the people from Madh.'

'She's already been introduced to the Master Sorcerer.'

'*Other* people.'

'*Why?*' Kalban asked, alarmed despite his cheerful mood. He couldn't think of any reason for Rati to want to meet magicians that wouldn't result in his being banished to the Eastern Isles. 'And *who*? The Head of the Inter-Realm Liaison Bureau?'

'I don't know. Stay and see what Rati wants before you go . . . I don't suppose you know what Mother's up to?'

'Is she up to something?'

'I know that tone. I'm going to find out, you know. You might as well tell me.'

'You probably *are* going to find out. It won't be *my* fault when you do. Thanks for letting me know about Rati. I'll talk to her today. I'm off.'

Kalban left, conscious of Abhinav's eyes on his back. While there was no longer open warfare between them, he wasn't foolish enough to imagine they were *friends*, not when they would one day be contending for the throne of Melucha. Despite what everyone said, Kalban knew that in Melucha itself, Abhinav had most of the advantages. It was refreshing to have the positions reversed.

As he passed through the entrance hall, Rati came out of an antechamber and stopped him.

'May I help you?' he said politely.

Rati considered him with a degree of interest that on any other day he would have found disconcerting.

'You *are* a different person here. I can see the appeal Madh had for you.'

'Can you?' Kalban was starting to feel wrong-footed.

'Yes. Melucha is, without question, the greatest nation in the world, but there's no denying that we're a bit insular. I expect you visited Rajgir often as a member of the Master Sorcerer's household.'

Kalban shrugged. 'More often than I would have done if I'd stayed in Melucha all my life.'

'Quite so. I want to speak to the Head of the Inter-Realm Liaison Bureau. When can you introduce me?'

Kalban hesitated. 'Hadn't you better ask my mother to introduce you? They're friends.'

'I'm asking *you*.'

'Do you want to come now? I'm going there anyway.'

'Certainly. Have you sent for the carriage?'

'We can walk,' Kalban said shortly. 'It's not far.'

'Ah, yes, I forgot that in Pür people walk on the public roads. How modern it all seems. Come along, then.'

At first, Kalban, to avoid awkward silence, pointed notable landmarks out to Rati as they walked. But after she assured him sweetly that she had been shown the Embassy of Vraja on the carriage ride from the Portals Hall, and she had little to no interest in the statue of the Rain God at the crossroads, he decided awkward silence was better.

'Madh has larger grounds than we do,' Rati observed disapprovingly as they walked through the gates. 'It's not even an independent country.'

'Madh has more people here than we do.'

The attendant at the door, recognizing Kalban, let them in without asking for identification. In response to Kalban's enquiry, he said most people were still at breakfast and in all likelihood Nalini was too.

Nalini emerged from the dining room as they were approaching it. Kalban wondered if the attendant had sent a message to her. As soon as Kalban had performed the necessary introduction, Nalini said, 'I can handle this now, thank you. Meenakshi was wondering when you'd be here.'

Meenakshi, seeing no sign of Gopali or Saha when she woke up, deduced that they had made themselves scarce to postpone the conversation about the books until after breakfast.

She hurried through it and returned to her room, meeting Kalban on the landing.

'I don't suppose you've had any luck,' he said when he saw her. 'You would have sent me a message.'

'Gopali confiscated the books.'

'*Why?* She's never confiscated anything, not even the copy of *The Summoner's Guide to Dangerous Yakshas* that you pretend not to have.'

'She's more concerned about the magical potential of the Fire of the East than about Yakshas.' Meenakshi opened her door and stepped in. 'Oh, *that's* an idea. We could Summon a Yaksha—much more efficient than searching for the gem ourselves—'

'We could *not*,' Kalban said, following her into the room and shutting the door. 'Leaving aside the small matter of *controlling* a Yaksha, that's an excellent way to make sure Rambha and Urvashi find out.'

'They're going to find out next week, if Nalini has to use the gem to get the Sprite back.'

'And this,' Gopali said, 'is why we should all stay out of this incipient disaster.' She was sitting where she had been the previous day, by the window. Saha wasn't there. Apparently, Gopali thought she was more than adequate to the task of browbeating Meenakshi. 'Do you really think it's a good idea to involve a Yaksha in this? If a mortal can't be trusted with the Fire of the East, do you think a *Yaksha* can? They're eight feet of pure rage!'

'A Yaksha that *we* Summoned—'

'Meenakshi, if the Fire of the East is everything it's rumoured to be, not even you can control a Yaksha who's got hold of it.'

'Wait,' Kalban said, 'how do you know so much about the Fire of the East?'

'I make it my business to know. And what were *you* thinking? You know this is stupid!'

'There's a Sprite missing in the Mortal Realm, and he might be dead in a week. The War of the Eight Djinn was started over less. Sprites might not be as powerful as Djinn, but they'll work together to avenge one of their own, which no Djinn ever did. As for the Fire of the East, if it's real, *if* it's everything that rumour says . . . I know it's dangerous. Short of going back in time and keeping Vasundhara from falling in love with a Sprite—'

'I suppose that's completely out of the question?' Gopali asked Meenakshi.

'*Now* who's not thinking?' Kalban demanded. 'At least, Nalini didn't suggest meddling with the fabric of reality!'

'We can't go back in time,' Meenakshi said regretfully. 'I don't know how—nobody's ever done it, and even if we could, we can't *undo* something that's already happened.'

'You could Scry,' suggested Gopali. 'That's the simplest way to find out who kidnapped him.'

'I've not worked out the time modification for Scrying into the past. Mother and Nalini and Kalban's mother are trying to find the Sprite. If they do, we won't need to give the gem to anyone.'

Gopali looked like she was wavering.

'I know this is irregular,' Kalban said, 'but it isn't a *secret* . . . it's just not yet been communicated to Rambha and Urvashi. Everyone else knows. The most powerful magicians of the Free Lands are all in Rajgir for the swayamvara. The *Master Sorcerer* is here. However this ends, it won't be with some power-mad kidnapper getting away with an arcane relic.'

Gopali sighed. 'Fine. You have to keep me informed of *everything*.' She held the books out to Meenakshi. 'Good luck.'

Meenakshi didn't start on the books as soon as Gopali left the room. While the answers to most questions could be found in books, she had a feeling that, if it were that simple, whoever they were looking for wouldn't have resorted to kidnapping a Sprite, a proceeding fraught with danger and almost certain to end in being handed over to Rambha and Urvashi to stand trial.

'All right,' said Kalban, when she said as much. 'You can read the books at night, anyway. No sense wasting daylight. Let's go see what's happening with the swayamvara.'

'How will that help?'

'All the court bards will be there. One of them might remember an old story about a magical gem.'

Meenakshi opened a portal. When Kalban glared at her, she said, 'It's all right! Didn't you get the pamphlet when you arrived? They've designated antechambers in the palace to open Mortal Realm portals for the duration of the swayamvara. They don't want all of us causing a pile-up on the main road.'

'They didn't tell us that.' Kalban shrugged. 'I suppose Melucha doesn't get the *interesting* tourist literature.'

'You've hardly brought anyone with you to need to use portals. Only Rati and Dev. And those people you don't like that you've badgered into humiliating themselves at the swayamvara.'

Meenakshi passed through the portal. Kalban followed.

The antechamber they stepped into was devoid of furnishings. The walls and floor were red stone, polished to a high, reflective shine.

Meenakshi let the portal close and hurried from the room. 'They're setting up the archery in the field by the river. Strictly speaking, I suppose we shouldn't see it, but you're not going to go and tell Melucha's entrants, are you?'

'Only if by doing so, I'd ruin their confidence.'

The sound of hammering guided them to the field beside the river. Normally used by the Maharaja's horse regiments for archery practice, it had been transformed past all recognition. When Kalban had last seen it, it had been an oval track for horses with targets in the middle and around the sides, plain dirt swept over as needed. The ground was now covered with a healthy growth of grass. Tiered stands for spectators had sprung up all around the field.

In the middle of the grass, several people were putting up what looked like a miniature defensive tower, complete with arrow-slits.

'There's Vasundhara,' said Kalban. 'I don't see any of the court bards.'

'Not trailing in the Princess's wake the day before the swayamvara? What a dereliction of duty. Will we have to come and watch tomorrow?'

'The search for the Fire of the East won't be admitted as an excuse,' Kalban said, as they walked across the grass. 'Not by Gopali.' He noticed that the blades sprang back perfectly straight, leaving no trace of their footsteps. All the minor magicians of Pür must have been hired for the swayamvara.

By then, Vasundhara had seen them, and stopped haranguing the carpenters long enough to wave.

'Wouldn't you know it?' she said when they were close enough. '*Months* to prepare, and we're still going to be hard at work the night before the event.'

'Have you heard from Ravi?' Meenakshi asked.

'No, I haven't. I've not had any more notes from the kidnapper, either. I don't mind telling you I'm concerned. Have you found anything?'

'We came here hoping your court bards might have some ideas of where the gem might be.'

'Where *are* the court bards?' said Kalban. 'Why aren't they here with you?'

'Grandfather has them in the Hall of Infinite Splendours,' Vasundhara said dismissively. 'He wants them to take notes so they don't miss out any important details when describing its splendours. They can just refer to the guide book, but it suits me. I don't need them all underfoot while I'm trying to get this set up—*you!*' she barked suddenly, making everyone else jump. 'You're hammering that plank in the wrong way!'

'We won't disturb you any more,' Kalban said carefully. 'You look far too busy—come on, Meenakshi. Let's go find the court bards. I'm sure they can take a few minutes off making notes about the Hall of Infinite Splendours.'

'Yes, all right,' said Vasundhara. 'You're coming tomorrow, Meenakshi, aren't you? I'll want you to help me set up the test for the afternoon.'

'Do you need *us* to help you?' asked Meenakshi. 'We thought we'd use the time to do some searching.'

'You can't. There'll be a delegation from the Inter-Realm and, *believe* me, they'll notice if the Master Sorcerer's daughter is missing at the exact time when a ransom demand has been made for a dangerous magical artefact. They'll be looking for you. See you tomorrow!'

Meenakshi and Kalban walked back across the wide sweep of lawn. As they neared the palace, an attendant ran up waving a letter.

'My lady!' He thrust it at Meenakshi. 'An urgent message.'

Meenakshi unfolded it and saw four words in Gopali's handwriting.

Come back at once.

CHAPTER IV

'I'm coming with you,' Kalban said, when Meenakshi showed him the note.

'Hadn't you better go to the Great Hall and speak to the minstrels?'

'You just want to get out of talking to them.'

'You *know* I'll just make them uncomfortable. You're better at that kind of thing.'

Kalban laughed. 'Fine. Go. I'll come and meet you there. And Meenakshi—'

'Don't do anything stupid. I know. Don't worry. I'm sure Gopali wants to give me a variant of that same lecture.'

Meenakshi opened a portal to the room set aside for that purpose in the High Commission of Madh. There was nobody on duty now that all expected guests had arrived. The halls were largely empty, most people having retired to their rooms after breakfast.

She was about to go upstairs when a voice said, 'Meenakshi! I hoped to see you.' Meenakshi turned.

Rati and Nalini were standing at the door to one of the rooms used to receive guests. 'Weddings are so delightful,' Rati went on, smiling. 'An unparalleled opportunity to meet old friends.'

Meenakshi eyed Rati doubtfully. She didn't actually *dislike* her as Kalban did, but calling her a *friend* was a stretch.

Fortunately, Nalini spared her the need to answer. 'Don't you have some reading to do, Meenakshi? Go on up.'

Meenakshi didn't need to be told twice. As she ran up the stairs, she heard Nalini say, 'Lady Rati, permit me to show you our library. We only keep a small collection here, but some books are *particularly* interesting . . . '

Meenakshi scoffed. From her experience, Nalini was quite as likely to give one a copy of the *By-laws of the International Code of Sorcery* as a book on Alchemical theory, and in both cases she would describe it as *interesting*.

'What is it?' she said as she opened the door to her room. 'I just went to the palace—'

Meenakshi stopped short. Gopali and Saha weren't alone. There was a woman with them, a beautiful woman with pearlescent skin, draped with a number of diaphanous silk scarves and dripping with bracelets and necklaces.

'*Chitralekha?*'

The Celestial Dancer smiled and said, in a voice that seemed offensively normal in comparison with her appearance, 'It's been *months* since I saw you. You're taller.'

'What are you doing here? How did you *get* here? Did you Summon her, Gopali?'

'I'm no magician. Nalini told me that Inter-Realm immigration regulations have been relaxed because of the swayamvara, so I sent her a message asking her to come.'

'*Why?*'

'It's nice to see you, too,' Chitralekha said. 'It's lucky I know you or I might be offended by your tone.'

'Yes, yes, I'm delighted and so on. May your shadow never grow less. Why *are* you here? Nobody's been murdered . . . ' She looked at Gopali. 'Have they?'

'No, nobody's been murdered. Having agreed to let you continue to search for the . . . ' She hesitated and glanced at Chitralekha. 'The Fire of the East—'

'You *told* her?' Meenakshi demanded, outraged. 'I *told* you Nalini didn't want Rambha and Urvashi to find out!'

'It was the only reasonable course of action, as you would realize yourself if you thought about it. If I can't dissuade you from doing this, you might as well do it with some hope of success. No mortal living knows anything other than rumour about the Fire of the East, but the Celestial Dancers have seen it.'

'She's right,' Chitralekha interrupted. 'And I won't tell Rambha or Urvashi . . . yet.'

'That's not reassuring.'

'The Celestial Dancers have seen the Fire of the East. *I've* seen the Fire of the East. It's . . . dangerous. Rajgir would be swarming with Dancers and Sprites in moments if Rambha and Urvashi found out you're looking for it.'

'Then—'

'I trust you . . . and Kalban. I don't know if I trust everyone *else* involved in this, which is all the more reason for me to be here to supervise.'

'You'll really help us?'

'That's why I'm here.'

'You won't tell anyone else?'

'Not unless you give me a reason to.'

Meenakshi sighed. She *knew* Kalban was going to have a lot to say about Chitralekha being involved in this, and he would say it at length and when she was trying to read. But there seemed to be no option.

'All right. What do you know about the Fire of the East?'

'Wait. There's something I want, too. Once this is over—the Sprite's been found and safely restored, a major Inter-Realm incident averted—I want your promise that you'll either destroy the Fire of the East, in front of me, or give it to the Dancers for safekeeping. It can't stay in the Mortal Realm.'

'I'm sure my father and Nalini will have something to say about what happens to it.'

'I'm sure the Master Sorcerer and the Head of the Inter-Realm Liaison Bureau will have their own ideas about what should be done with the Fire of the East. I'm sure they'll mean well.'

'How do you know the gem will be safe in the Inter-Realm?'

'It'll be in the Dancers' vault, which is as secure as anything *can* be in any realm. If you have your doubts—I don't blame you if you do—then destroy it.'

'Destroy it,' Meenakshi repeated slowly. 'That would be difficult, to deliberately *destroy* something like that. I don't know if I could. But I'll give it to you.'

'Then I'll tell you what I know. The gem passed through several hands until Tara the Starchaser got hold of it on her travels—'

'Mother was right!'

'I'm not surprised. Your mother knows more old stories than any mortal should. Tara used the gem, often—and several Dancers were in the Mortal Realm, *often*, because of her. I was one of them. Luckily, she wasn't actually powerful enough to be a threat—'

'I thought she was a rival of the Great Sorceress Anasuya.'

'Not even close. Her descendants, being the rulers of Pür, propagated that legend. Tara was clever, yes, and resourceful, but only marginally more talented at magic than your uncle.'

Meenakshi's uncle Asmanjas had been the first child of the family in generations with no gift for magic. He was wont to say that there had been no room left for magic because he had been given triple the normal allowance of common sense.

Chitralekha continued, 'Her great-grandson Amsuman had no magical ability at all, so he was quite willing to sell everything he inherited from her to the highest bidder.'

'Everything?'

'*Almost* everything. Naturally, we couldn't let dangerous magical artefacts fall into the wrong hands. This was before the signing of the Inter-Realm Accord, so we had to do things the old-fashioned way. We tracked people down and retrieved most of the cache. There were a few items we never were able to trace.

Urvashi went to Amsuman herself to find out who had them. He told her *he* had them still.'

'Was he telling the truth?'

'*Nobody* can lie to Urvashi.'

'Did she let him keep them?'

'She didn't want to. He claimed he'd already put them in a secret, secure location. He'd begun to realize his folly by then—the relics were useless to him, but not to magicians. When he understood that he was giving other people power he'd never have, he was happy to help us. But . . . he had his quirks. He wouldn't tell Urvashi *where* he'd put his remaining treasures, but he promised to leave her a clue in his will.'

'I take it he didn't.'

'We never found out. When he died, his children fought one another for the throne. In the process, his will was lost before any of us had a chance to look at it. Rambha and Urvashi decided it was safest to let the matter rest . . . And they weren't wrong. Five hundred years, and not a whisper of the Fire of the East.'

'Until now.'

Chitralekha nodded. 'Until now.'

Kalban, in the Hall of Infinite Splendours, was feeling irritable.

His mood would have horrified the original architect, who had conceived an airy room with a high ceiling meant to elevate the spirits, and the subsequent artists who had covered the walls in murals depicting fanciful (Chitralekha would have complained, inaccurate) scenes from the history of the Inter-Realm for the same purpose.

There was a mixed crowd in the Hall. The Yaunic Ambassador, white-robed like a philosopher, which Kalban knew was only an affectation, rubbed shoulders with the High Lord of Vraja, clad in gold-plated armour. A few Sprites, whether in Rajgir to search for their missing friend or to attend the swayamvara, Kalban didn't know, sampled the snacks that were borne in by silent attendants. Courtiers and nobles from around Pür clustered in small groups to exchange the latest news.

The minstrels, aware of their audience and hoping for patronage, kept up a steady stream of light music. Kalban's attempts to get their attention went unheeded. Those who did know him as the elder but less favoured son of the Prince Regnant of Melucha had last seen him when he was that lowest of all created beings, a Sorcerer's apprentice.

Kalban, after a moment's hesitation, decided there was no point trying to distract them from their determined odes in praise of the various rulers. He looked around the room to see if there was anybody else who might help him. Bahuka, the Minister for Inter-Realm Affairs, gave him an affable nod.

Kalban approached Bahuka and explained his requirement in an undertone. Bahuka shook his head regretfully.

'It won't work. Whoever has the Sprite must already have looked into old songs and stories. Kidnapping Sprites is something you only do as a last resort.' He paused. 'You might want to discuss it with your father or your brother. Perhaps what this needs is an outsider's perspective . . . someone who doesn't know much of Rajgir or of magic.'

Kalban left the room, the singing, and the inane advice of someone who clearly knew nothing of Melucha or Kalban's family, whatever he might know of Rajgir and magic.

$\maltese$

Nalini looked at the imposing edifice before her, not in the least intimidated. The estate of Lord Das was outside the city—Nalini's horse was being rubbed down and fed by Lord Das's head stable hand—and the property covered several acres. Lord Das had bought the land recently, when the discovery of an ancient treasure hoard in a cave on his country estate had elevated his financial position beyond that of most minor nobles.

The new proprietor had then *improved* the land—although not in Nalini's view—by the addition of what could only be described as a miniature fortress. It was equipped with turrets, battlements, the portcullis through which she had just passed, and buttresses both normal and flying. Every space on the walls where a statue could possibly fit was occupied by a bygone monarch of Pür.

Before she could reach for the bell-pull beside the fifteen-foot-high front door, the door opened.

Nalini believed in dressing for her job. As Head of the Inter-Realm Liaison Bureau, that meant enough gold and gemstones at wrists and throat to buy, if not Lord Das's entire castle, at least one excessively ornate wing. The attendant who opened the door took in her silks and jewellery and said, in a tone of considerably more respect than he might otherwise have used, 'May I have your name, my lady?'

'The Head of the Inter-Realm Liaison Bureau. I'm here to speak to Lord Das.'

'Please come in.' The attendant led her to a drawing room that commanded a glorious view of the garden, where the hand of Man had done everything possible to tame the glories of nature. 'Please wait here. I'll inform Lord Das.'

Nalini looked around the room. Secret passages and hidden chambers were out of fashion these days. Most newer constructions lacked them. But she'd be willing to bet a lot of money—or at least a considerable amount of djinn gold—that Lord Das's residence had as many as all the rest of Rajgir put together. There were several likely-looking bookcases and a fireplace large enough for six people to hold a clandestine meeting.

The attendant returned.

'Lord Das sends his apologies, my lady. He is indisposed. He deeply regrets that he must miss the opportunity to speak to you. He begs you to partake of the hospitality of the house before you leave.'

'That won't be necessary,' Nalini said, smiling. 'I'm so sorry to hear Lord Das is unwell. I don't want to disturb him—I'm sure he must be resting quietly in the hope of being able to attend the opening of the swayamvara tomorrow. There's no need to bother him. I just want to search the house.'

'One moment, my lady.'

The attendant disappeared. This time he was gone for several minutes.

When he returned, his demeanour had undergone a change. 'Forgive me, my lady,' he said coldly. 'Lord Das regrets that he is unable to accommodate your request. Good day.'

'It wasn't a request,' Nalini said cheerfully. 'I have a search and seizure order signed by the Maharaja.' She held it up so the attendant could see the seal. When he reached for it, she snatched it back. 'I'll hold on to it. It would be tragic if an accident befell the order while you took it to Lord Das. You go and report to him. I'll wait here.'

'Perhaps, my lady, you could come back later on and conduct your search when Lord Das is feeling better. This evening would be suitable.'

'Are you sure that's wise? I wouldn't want to do *anything* to hinder Lord Das's ability to attend the swayamvara tomorrow— and, you see, if I leave now and come back this evening, it's likely that Lady Kamakshi and Princess Persis of Melucha will come with me. That would be so disruptive to the household. Did you know that Kamakshi has spent several years studying the magical wildlife of the Eastern Isles?'

'The Eastern Isles? There are chimeras there!'

'So people say. Kamakshi will have more information on the subject. You can ask her this evening. Persis, on the other hand, knows very little about magical animals.'

'*Ah,*' said in the attendant, in a tone that suggested that he was prepared to like Princess Persis.

'She prefers *normal* animals. When we were students at the Academy, she perfected a spell to turn people into pigs.'

'*Oh,*' he said, a definite change from *Ah.*

'If you're certain that's what Lord Das would like, I'll be on my way.'

'Just a moment, my lady. I'll go and . . . ascertain his preference.'

'Just as you please,' Nalini said equably.

CHAPTER V

Kalban thought he must be seeing things. It was a mirage, or an optical illusion, or possibly a figment of his imagination brought on by the minstrels' interminable songs about fair maidens disporting themselves on riverbanks. It *had* to be one of those things, because the alternative was that a Celestial Dancer—a Celestial Dancer they knew, yes, but still an immortal being who must be kept *out* of this—was sitting in Meenakshi's room petting the griffon.

'What are *you* doing here?'

'Hello,' said Chitralekha, proving that she was real and not a mirage, optical illusion or figment of Kalban's imagination. 'Are you having a nice time in Rajgir? Isn't it usually Meenakshi who skips the pleasantries?'

'You *can't* be here!'

'Normally, no. Immigration rules have been relaxed because of the swayamvara. Meenakshi knows I'm here.'

'Where's Meenakshi?'

'Here,' said Meenakshi's voice from behind him. He turned to see her entering the room with a rolled-up scroll. 'Did you have any luck with the minstrels?'

'Not to speak of. What's that? What's Chitralekha doing here? Did you . . . ' He pulled Meenakshi aside and dropped his voice. 'Did you *tell* her?'

'Gopali did. Don't worry. She's going to help us.' Meenakshi went to her desk. 'Shut the door. I need to unroll this. I don't want a draught.'

Kalban shut the door. Meenakshi rolled the paper out on the desk.

'Family tree of the royal family of Pür,' she explained. 'I didn't have to go to the library for it. There was one downstairs.'

'What are we looking for?' Chitralekha asked.

'*Wait*,' Kalban said. 'Why are you helping us?'

'I've taken a liking to the two of you. I want to keep you out of trouble if I can.' Chitralekha paused. 'And Meenakshi promised that after it's over she'll give me the Fire of the East. Honestly, I'd rather she destroyed it, but it's still a better option than having it knocking about loose in the Mortal Realm for the next dark sorcerer to find.'

'*And*, which you just happened to overlook mentioning, if you're the one responsible for taking it to Rambha, you'll get *another* promotion.'

'You're one to talk,' Chitralekha said. '*You're* doing it because it'll make you look good to the Privy Council if you've had a hand in resolving what might have been a major diplomatic disaster— and Meenakshi's curious about the gem and wants to see it for herself. None of us is here for the sake of the greater good. Now that we've established that, what are we looking for?'

'I don't know,' Meenakshi said. 'Anything interesting. Anyone who pops out at you for some reason—did anything unusual—someone everyone loved or everyone hated.'

'I don't know how you define *unusual*,' Kalban said. 'The present Maharaja is alleged to have murdered thirty-seven people to take the throne.'

'And now the most exciting part of his day is choosing which brocade he wants each morning,' said Chitralekha. 'How the mighty have fallen.'

⁂

Lord Das padded into the room wrapped in a blue shawl, clutching a hot-water bottle. His face had an unhealthy pallor, which Nalini's experienced eye judged as being caused by the judicious application of face paint. His eyes were bright and alert.

'Lord Das,' Nalini said. 'I'm so sorry to hear you're unwell. There was no need for you to trouble yourself to come downstairs. I'm sure your staff could have provided everything.'

'I couldn't forgo the chance of speaking to such an illustrious visitor myself. My wife and children will be sorry to have missed you.'

'I trust they're enjoying themselves at the festivities.'

'My household is at your disposal. We would not dream of disregarding the Maharaja's search and seizure order. My only regret is that we did not have more notice so that we could have had everything ready for you.'

'Since you *are* here, Lord Das, perhaps we could speak in private?' Lord Das nodded to the attendant, who disappeared. 'Thank you. I'm sure you know why I'm here.'

'I am at a loss.'

'Lord Das, we must be honest with each other. I know you've been having a house guest.'

'Naturally, when my cousins are in Rajgir I'm happy to—'

'I'm sure you are.' Nalini allowed a distinct hard edge to creep into her voice. She was a magician, after all, and a highly competent one. 'You know who I am, I take it, Lord Das.'

'Who has not heard of—'

'I am the *Head* of the Inter-Realm Liaison Bureau. For *all* of Pür. I *know* you had a Sprite staying with you for over a month. That Sprite has now disappeared. You're going to tell me everything you know about it, right here in your drawing room while we look at this nice view of the lawn.'

'If I refuse, you're going to ask Princess Persis to turn me into a pig?'

'Certainly not. We're not *barbarians*. There are *laws* in Pür. If you refuse, I'm going to follow the proper procedure, which would be to register a complaint. One does hope that the Maharaja's Complaints Tribunal wouldn't go to the extreme of seizing your estate pending resolution of the matter. Who can say how official channels will run?'

'Are you threatening me?'

'I'm not *threatening* anything. Civilization has progressed beyond that stage.'

'Fine,' grunted Lord Das. 'Sit down. I'll call for wine.'

'Tell me,' Chitralekha said, 'just *why* are we going back to the library?' She was almost running to keep up, snatching at her scarves to prevent them from drifting on to the road. 'Slow down! There's no hurry!'

'You're having a hard time because of all those bits of floaty material,' Meenakshi said. 'Get rid of them. You were fine in Melucha.'

'Not unless there's a reason! This is Rajgir. I might meet someone I know.'

'You said Amsuman's granddaughter Lilavati only reigned for eight days before she was deposed by her cousin and she went into a comfortable exile.'

'Much more comfortable than the cousin who deposed her or the country she left behind,' Kalban supplied.

'Yes, I did—oh, I'm *so* sorry,' said Chitralekha, as the tasseled end of a scarf floated into the face of a passing horse. 'How well-trained your horse is,' she added to the irate rider. 'He didn't even throw you. I know what you're thinking, Meenakshi.' Chitralekha wound the ends of her scarves around her wrist to hold them in place. 'What if she found the treasure and took it with her? What does that have to do with the library?'

'There was a collection of her letters.'

'Yes, and I read them,' Kalban said. 'There's nothing to suggest the location of Amsuman's treasure.'

'You didn't know yesterday who she was or that she might have had it. We need to read those letters again.' Meenakshi stopped at an intersection to let a procession go past. Judging by the crocodiles waddling on leashes at the edges of it, causing passers-by to step well back and mutter about dangerous animal regulations, it must be from Vraja. 'What *is* this? *They're* allowed to have crocodiles on the street and I have to keep the griffon shut in my room?'

'Crocodiles aren't unnatural beasts created by Alchemy,' Chitralekha said.

'I'm sure that'll be comforting when you get eaten by one,' Kalban said. As the last juggler went by and they crossed the street, he added, 'We'll have to be quick. It's the opening ceremony this afternoon. I need to be there—and so do you, Meenakshi.'

'We know the book. It won't take long.'

Meenakshi slowed down as they neared the library gate. Several Sprites were standing in a tight knot just outside it, scanning the faces of all who passed.

'I'll join you in a few minutes,' Chitralekha murmured, falling back. 'They can't know I'm helping you.'

Meenakshi would have walked past the Sprites, but one of them stepped directly into her path.

'Move aside,' Meenakshi ordered, looking up into his face.

Inhuman, glittering eyes met hers. 'How courteous. Did nobody teach you that requests should be phrased politely?'

'I'm not stupid enough to give you a loophole. It wasn't a request. Move *aside.*'

'You're not my Summoner.'

The Sprite reached out as though to seize Meenakshi's arm, but one of his companions hastily pulled him back.

'Lay hands on a magician and that'll be all the excuse they need! This isn't the time to start a public brawl.'

'When does a public brawl become a battle?' snarled the first one. 'If Ravi is harmed, it will be time to find out. We won't hold back if magicians allow one of their own to kill one of us. Remember that, girl.'

Meenakshi stepped around him and went on down the path.

The basement room was as dim and stuffy as it had been the previous day. Meenakshi, instead of asking one of the clerks for a torch, conjured a lamp, responding to Kalban's warning with, 'Don't *worry*. It's safer than a torch. Nobody's even going to notice I did it.'

'She's right,' Chitralekha said, appearing in the doorway. 'With all the magicians in Rajgir right now, this won't be a blip on the sensor. I saw those Sprites speaking to another magician after you came inside. Yaunic, by the look of him.'

'What does it mean when they say they won't hold back?' Kalban asked. 'They can't really be thinking of attacking magicians? Now, in Rajgir, with everyone here, they'd be bound to lose.'

'Sprites are notoriously irrational,' Chitralekha said, but without the dismissive tone that characterized most of her comments about Sprites. 'They don't care about losing a fight. They would be delighted if the Inter-Realm Accord ended. They hate the power it gives Rambha and Urvashi.'

'Here's the book.' Meenakshi pulled it from the shelf and gave it to Kalban. 'You know it best. Read it, and I'll try to find something else.'

Kalban forced his mind away from visions of Sprites battling magicians in the streets. 'What are you looking for?'

'Another book about Lilavati. There must have been *some* minstrel or court bard who wanted to write about the eight days' maharani . . . her name on an old map . . . anything.'

Kalban opened the book.

'You won't find anything,' said Chitralekha. 'I *knew* Lilavati. She wasn't the type to keep her treasure a secret. If she'd had it, believe me, *everyone* would have known about it. She would have been as famous as Tara the Starchaser.'

'Lilavati was a magician?' Meenakshi asked, taking books down at random from the shelves.

'I didn't say she was.'

'Why else would you know her?'

Chitralekha shrugged. 'We weren't sure the Fire of the East *had* disappeared. She wasn't powerful enough to worry anyone. I was very junior then, remember. If they'd thought she was a serious risk, I wouldn't have got the job.'

'And look at you now, conducting independent murder investigations and . . . whatever it is you're doing here.' Meenakshi shoved the books back. 'Right, what *was* the source of Lilavati's wealth in exile?'

'According to this letter,' Kalban said, 'she married a rich man who wanted to be able to boast that his children were descendants of Tara the Starchaser.'

Meenakshi made a face, and pushed the next book, a particularly heavy volume, back with unnecessary vim. One of the bricks in the wall behind it shifted just a hair.

Meenakshi stopped and stared at it.

She reached around the books to give the brick another tentative push.

There was definite movement.

Meenakshi pulled a dozen books off the shelf and shoved them haphazardly onto the one below. Barely visible in the light of the lamp, the brick wasn't aligned with the others.

'What is it?' Chitralekha said.

Meenakshi turned to Kalban. 'You're the expert on secret compartments. Come and look at this.'

Kalban came.

'I need more light.'

Meenakshi conjured a half-dozen lamps that clustered around them. The stuffy space grew uncomfortably warm.

Kalban ran his fingers over the brick, probing carefully until, with a high-pitched grinding noise that Meenakshi was *certain* would bring the clerks down on them, it came away from the wall. Kalban laid it on the shelf.

Behind it was a dark recess.

'Booby-trapped?' he asked.

Meenakshi probed it with magic. A tiny jet of brick dust spurted from a corner of the recess.

'Probably poison originally,' Chitralekha observed. 'It must have evaporated.'

'All the same, I don't want to stick my hand inside,' Kalban said.

'Nor do I,' said Chitralekha.

Meenakshi made an impatient noise and waved at the recess. A cloud of dust rose into the air, making her and Kalban cough. When it settled, a small wooden box floated through the air. The lid was carved with a pattern of elephants and mangoes.

'That's in *excellent* condition,' Chitralekha murmured, 'considering that it's been there long enough for the poison to dry up.'

'That's because someone cast a preservation spell on it . . . to protect whatever's inside.' Meenakshi floated the box over to the table. Then she hesitated. 'It'll break the spell to open it.'

'And whatever's inside will crumble to dust?' asked Chitralekha.

'No, it'll be fine. It'll *start* to age normally.'

'You can cast another spell if we need to. Open it and see.'

The lid came off.

There was a sheet of paper inside, folded.

'Don't touch,' Meenakshi said. 'It may be fragile.'

'It may be *poisoned*,' Kalban said.

The paper floated out of the box and unfolded itself on the table.

Meenakshi, Kalban and Chitralekha stared at it in silence. Then Chitralekha said, 'I don't know how well up the two of you are on ancient scripts—'

'Five hundred years old isn't *ancient*,' Meenakshi said dismissively.

'I know more ancient languages than modern ones,' Kalban said. 'One of the perks of having had my early education at the hands of a classical philosopher.'

'So . . .' Chitralekha paused. 'We all know what we're looking at.'

'Amsuman's will,' Kalban said.

'With the alleged location of his treasure,' Chitralekha specified.

Meenakshi laughed. 'We're going treasure-hunting!'

CHAPTER VI

'I don't know who took the Sprite. I didn't have anything to do with it.' Lord Das waved his hands in what seemed to Nalini to be exaggerated exasperation. 'Why would I want that sort of trouble?'

'There's been a ransom demand.'

'I'm not desperate for money. Look around you! Those are real gold threads in the carpet. I don't want my house being overrun by Celestial Dancers searching for clues . . . I try to be tolerant, but the rest of Pür, as I'm sure you're aware, isn't as used to being a thoroughfare for the Inter-Realm as Madh is. Where I come from, there was a part of the forest nobody entered because of a rumour that a Yakshini *might* live there. An infestation of Dancers would be *worse* than Yakshas. On that subject, where are they?'

'Where are Yakshas?'

'Where are all your searchers? Do you intend to comb through my entire house by yourself? That doesn't seem to be a productive use of time for the *Head* of the Inter-Realm Liaison Bureau. For all of Pür.'

'How careless of me,' Nalini said. 'I forgot to bring anyone with me. We'll remedy that, shall we?' She looked around. 'Not here . . . I wouldn't want an accident to your carpet. The passage outside, perhaps?'

Without waiting for an answer, she went to the door and flung it wide. Waving away the attendant who sprang forward, she opened a portal.

Two by two, eight figures came through. Four were human, two were Sprites, one a Celestial Dancer, and there was one whose species Lord Das could not have guessed if he had been offered another ancient treasure. It was clear that they had all been waiting for the summons.

'Since portals regulations have been relaxed,' Nalini said, 'it seemed unkind to tire eight additional horses for no reason. I came the old-fashioned way, so that we wouldn't startle you by opening a portal onto your lawn. Having so graciously consented to cooperate, I'm sure you'll have no objection to our beginning without delay.'

'Oh,' Lord Das said unhappily.

He signalled to the waiting attendant, who said in a voice that at once conveyed deference and well-bred distaste, 'This way, please,' and led the new arrivals down the passage.

'My staff will show your friends everything they wish,' Lord Das assured Nalini.

'I would expect no less. While your staff are assisting with the search, let's continue our discussion.' Nalini marched back into the library and seated herself on one of the padded couches. 'You were telling me your views on who kidnapped Ravi.'

'I'm telling you I have no idea. The day he disappeared, we had no unexpected visitors. He seemed normal in the morning—dug into his breakfast—spoke about his training. He was concerned that there should be no doubts cast on his victory—'

'He *was* confident of victory, then?'

Lord Das gave an impatient shrug. 'It's a swayamvara, and we all know that Princess Vasundhara is a young woman who knows her own mind. She would have made certain of it.'

'I suppose so. Go on.'

'That's all. He didn't come to lunch. I didn't think anything of it—he didn't always eat every meal.'

'Eating is optional for Sprites,' Nalini agreed.

'When he didn't come to dinner, I sent someone up to look for him. They found no trace—no signs of a struggle. Nobody saw him leave, but that doesn't mean he didn't. This is a *house*, not a prison. We don't keep watch on the doors.'

'So you're telling me he left willingly with his kidnapper?'

'That, or the kidnapper was never on the premises at all. Ravi might have gone for a walk—or to practise riding. He'd been doing that. He has a fine seat on a horse, you know. Very proud of it—and indeed he *will* be an asset on the parade ground.'

Nalini couldn't decide if Lord Das was being deliberately obstructionist. Fortunately, she was spared the need to probe further. There was a commotion outside the door and one of the Sprites on her team burst in.

'My lord, I tried to stop him,' wailed the attendant hurrying in his wake. 'He wouldn't wait—'

'We don't have time to waste,' the Sprite said imperatively. 'Come upstairs.'

⚜

Expecting to be shown to an antechamber to wait, Abhinav was surprised when, without even asking for his name, the man at the door—Abhinav would have called him a guard but he didn't have even a *ceremonial* sword—pointed to the large staircase.

'The Master Sorcerer's daughter. Three floors up, turn left, fifth door down. While we will make all efforts to prevent damage to your person, we do not guarantee your safety. Proceed at your own risk. Where are you from?'

'I'm from Melucha,' said Abhinav. 'Aren't you going to make certain I don't have weapons?'

'You are now in the territory of Madh,' said the man, looking at him as though uncertain of his wits. 'If you attack a practitioner of magic through means magical or otherwise, you automatically forfeit all right to legal recourse. Proceed at your own risk. Do you wish to enter?'

'I'll find my own way up.'

Other than the occasional curious glance, nobody paid Abhinav any attention. He followed the guard's directions and found himself facing a door that had nothing to distinguish it from the other doors up and down the corridor.

He knocked.

Something inside the room screeched.

Abhinav took a step back and was standing away from the door when it opened. Kalban stood in the doorway, taking up as much of it as possible. Over his shoulder, Abhinav could see Meenakshi and Chitralekha hastily rolling up some documents and stowing them in a chest.

There was another screech.

'Oh, be quiet,' Meenakshi said, looking at something Abhinav couldn't see. Then she added, 'Let him in, it's fine.'

'Is it?' Abhinav asked cautiously.

'The griffon?' Kalban said, with a smile that wasn't entirely devoid of malice. 'You're not *scared* of it, surely?'

Abhinav glared at him and stalked into the room, in time to see Chitralekha pushing a box under the bed. An animal was lying on its back on the floor beside the bed. If that was a griffon, it was far smaller than Abhinav would have expected. He had an impression of mismatched legs and feathers; then it rolled over and stretched its wings. Suddenly, it was looming alarmingly large.

'Here.' Chitralekha flung open a door Abhinav hadn't noticed, in the wall beside the desk. 'If he makes you nervous, just go in there. He won't follow unless Meenakshi calls him. Too much magic.'

Deciding that, on balance, magic made him less nervous than the griffon, Abhinav took her advice.

He found himself in a small room that contained a table and chairs, a small shelf in one corner and a white-painted pentagram on the floor. Other than the pentagram, it might have been the study of a particularly austere student in Melucha. Other than the pentagram . . . and the feeling that something was tickling every exposed bit of skin.

He shivered.

'That's the magic,' Kalban said, joining him. 'You'll get used to it—or not. Why are you here?'

'Do you know what's happening?'

'I can't say anything. I told you already.'

'They're saying that a Sprite's been murdered.' There was a pause. Abhinav stared at his brother. 'It's *true*?'

'Of course, it's not true,' Chitralekha said sharply. '*Who's* saying a Sprite's been murdered?'

'People. Rumour. The word on the street. If it isn't true, then what *is* happening? *Who's* been murdered?'

'Nobody's been murdered,' said Chitralekha. 'This isn't Melucha.'

'As far as we know,' Meenakshi added. 'About the murder, I mean.'

'Yes, thank you. Nobody's been murdered *as far as we know*. If that's all you were here for, you have your answer. Goodbye.'

'I'm not going anywhere until I know what's happening.' Abhinav sat in one of the chairs to emphasize his point. 'Maybe I can help.' When Kalban looked pointedly at the pentagram on the ground, Abhinav rolled his eyes and said, 'I didn't say I could help with magic. I can run interference with Rati, if you want to keep her from learning too much.'

Chitralekha and Meenakshi came into the study.

'What does Rati know?' Chitralekha asked.

'She knows something's up, just like everyone who's not a complete fool. How secret can you be when there are Dancers and Sprites in force all over the city?'

'Fine,' Chitralekha said. 'I'll tell you what you *need* to know. A Sprite's disappeared. I don't suppose there's any harm in telling you *that*. It'll be common knowledge when he doesn't show up for the first contest tomorrow.'

'For the contest? Wait—the Sprite that Princess Vasundhara wants to marry? The intended consort to the future Maharani of Pür? *He's* disappeared?'

'We're all trying to find him—through different means. Your mother included. That's all you need to know.'

'There must be *something* I can do.'

'Stay out of the way,' Chitralekha said. 'That's what you can do. The last thing this situation needs is somebody who can't defend himself—'

'I'm a prince of Melucha,' Abhinav said, stung. 'I've been trained in four types of martial arts.'

'Much good will those do you against magical adversaries. You can't help.' Chitralekha's voice took on a commanding note. '*Go home.*'

Nalini stood in the middle of the bedroom.

Like the rest of the house, the bedroom that Ravi had used was on a lavish scale. But it wasn't the silk curtains with gold tassels or the thick rugs that made Nalini stand perfectly still, her fingers spread as though trying to catch an invisible breeze.

'Well?' asked the young man anxiously.

'You could be right. I can't say for certain.' She looked at the Sprite who had called her from the library. 'Go stand guard. Don't let anyone else from the household come in.' The Sprite left at once. Nalini turned to the young man. 'Go to the other end of the house—or better yet, go outside to the lawn—and open a portal to the High Commission. Bring Kamakshi. If she's not there, bring Paras.'

'What if the Master Sorcerer is busy, my lady?' the youth asked hesitantly. Madh was rife with tales of what happened to people who disturbed the Master Sorcerer when he was busy.

'It doesn't matter. This is *important*. Tell him I said so.'

'Hadn't I better fetch Meenakshi instead?'

Nalini considered for a moment. Then she shook her head. 'Don't do that. Just go and get Kamakshi or Paras. Hurry. The magical signatures won't last much longer. While you're going, tell everyone no more magic in the house. I don't want any conflicting signals.'

Left alone, Nalini looked around the room. She didn't expect physical clues—in all likelihood, the room had been cleaned already—and there *were* none. There was also, she noted, opening a cupboard, nothing that might have belonged to Ravi. Sprites were notorious hoarders; it was inconceivable that one had occupied this room for an extended period and not filled it with odd knick-knacks and bits of jewellery.

She stepped out of the room. 'Bharga!' The Sprite keeping guard turned to look at her. 'Send someone to Das to ask him what he's done with the Sprite's things.'

She re-entered the room.

In a few minutes there was a sharp, impatient knock. The door was opened without waiting for an answer. Paras bustled in.

Contrary to every rule of art or literature, the Master Sorcerer was a tall, energetic man who appeared every inch the most powerful magician of the Free Lands. No unwary enemy was likely to overlook Paras under the impression that he was a mild-mannered clerk or a penniless vagrant.

'What is it?' Paras said gruffly. 'Your man said it was important and Asamanjas made me come.'

Contrary to every rule of art or literature, the Master Sorcerer could be successfully bullied by completely unmagical people if, like his brother, they knew the right way to go about it.

'It *is* important,' Nalini said. 'Can you sense the residual magic in this room?'

'Faintly. Why?'

'Human or Immortal?'

'Both. *Why?*'

'This was the Sprite's room. What was the magic?'

Paras walked slowly into the middle of the room. He didn't try to feel the air as Nalini had done. He didn't need to.

'There was a Sprite here. And there's mortal magic. I can't tell whose. There aren't any real signatures from the mortal.' Paras looked around the room. 'Because the human never stood in this room. It was Summoning magic. The Sprite resisted.' Paras stepped back, crouched, and flung back the rug. A large scorch mark marred the marble floor. 'Ultimately, the Sprite answered the Summons.'

Nalini let out a breath and knelt to look. 'I thought as much. Was he harmed?'

'Probably not.' Paras traced the scorch mark with one hand. 'This would just have been his magic burning out against the Summons. No lasting damage.'

'Can you tell how long ago it happened?'

'It might be anything from a day to a week. It depends on the power of the caster. I suppose you'll ask the Dancers to check everyone's magical output.'

'I will, for all the good it'll do. It doesn't take a lot of magic to Summon a Sprite. A first-year student might do it. And since we can't even really narrow down the time . . . It does tell us one thing,' Nalini said, getting to her feet. 'There's a mortal magician involved.'

Abhinav was in the Embassy of Melucha before his head cleared.

As soon as it did, he was furious. He understood that as a foreigner he might not be informed of everything that happened in Pür, particularly when it concerned the Inter-Realm, with which Melucha had little traffic. He even understood, although it galled him, that Kalban was likelier to get the truth, given his history with all parties involved.

To be compelled to stop asking questions by a Celestial Dancer was *insupportable*.

Abhinav went to his room, took down a book, and began to make notes.

CHAPTER VII

A heavy fist thudded against the door. A voice bellowed, 'Thirty minutes!'

Meenakshi, trying to read a book while simultaneously mending a button that had inexplicably broken in her trunk, groaned.

'Why need we have all this *pageantry*? It's not even a *real* contest.'

'Because people *like* it,' Gopali said briskly. She took the blouse from Meenakshi. 'Give me that. Even if the conclusion is foregone, the competition is exciting. Put the book away. You can't bring a book to the opening event of the swayamvara. Everyone will cheer for their chosen candidate, *even* if they know there's no chance. Saha, do you have the flowers?'

'Here,' said Saha. She, like Gopali, was already fully dressed, down to fine jewelled bangles clasped around her wrists.

Meenakshi shut the book and laid it on the table. 'I don't see why I have to go. This is more important than a social event.'

'Two reasons. First, your mother and Nalini won't be there, since they're trying to work out who could have Summoned Ravi from Lord Das's house. Your skirt needs to be an inch higher or you're going to trip over it. Unless we want Madh to make a poor showing and offend Princess Vasundhara, you need to go.'

'Vasundhara won't be offended. She knows what's happening.'

'That brings me to the second reason. As far as *you* are concerned, nothing is happening. Princess Vasundhara knows the truth. Most people don't. Bangles. We have to keep it that way. Not just one bangle. I said *bangles*. I heard Rambha herself might attend the opening of the swayamvara. She *will* notice if you're not there. That means you're going, and not poring over an ancient atlas while you're there. Earrings.'

'You're making me conspicuous,' Meenakshi complained, when Saha gave her a ruby necklace.

'When Rambha sees you, you need to look like a young lady who's been spending the last two days planning her dress for the greatest social event of the year, not like we had to forcibly separate you from a search for an illegal artefact and stuff you into respectable clothes.'

'We need to go over the guests.' Gopali thrust a sheet of paper under Meenakshi's nose. 'We haven't much time. They've put you next to the Yaunic Ambassador. That's fortunate. He has no objection to magic and he's fond of mathematics and philosophy. And there's nobody from Yauna competing so you're unlikely to offend him. On the other side, there's one of the young ladies of court—from Pür,' Gopali added. 'Just be polite. It'll be fine.'

'Have a quick look who's in the row behind you,' Saha said, looking over Meenakshi's shoulder at the chart. 'Even if you won't be expected to make conversation with them, they'll hear what you're saying to the others. Some minor lords from Vraja just behind you . . . '

The lecture went on until the thump on the door came again, this time with the information that it was time to go.

Meenakshi, Gopali and Saha went downstairs. For efficiency, a single portal had been opened to the palace. They joined the line.

In a few minutes, they were emerging on the lawn and Gopali was pointing Meenakshi to the enclosure where she would find her seat.

'Where will you be?' Meenakshi asked.

'Luckily for us, since *we're* neither the daughters of the Governor nor potentially powerful future magicians, Saha and I can mingle with the crowd. We're going to meet some friends. Go and enjoy yourself.'

'Don't be rude to anyone,' Saha added.

With a sigh, Meenakshi went in. Vasundhara, waiting at the entrance, drew her aside. 'Well?' she said in an undertone. 'Have you found anything?'

'We've found . . . a map, I suppose. We're working on it. I was hoping to this morning—'

'*Much* better not,' Vasundhara said. 'You need some time away from these things. It'll clear your head. Ugh,' she added when a young man, who looked vaguely familiar to Meenakshi, approached them with hands outstretched. 'There's that frightful bore from Vraja. I'd better talk to him. You go sit. I asked them to put you next to the Yaunic Ambassador.'

'Yes, I saw.'

'He *loves* magic,' Vasundhara said. 'No good at it, but he talks about it almost as enthusiastically as he does about poison. He asked to sit next to your father. Nobody wanted to take *that* risk. Just talk to him about Summoning and that poisoning business in Melucha last year and you won't have any trouble.'

Leaving Vasundhara to the Vraja contingent, Meenakshi went in search of her seat.

The Yaunic Ambassador hadn't yet arrived. A young woman was sitting in the seat on the other side of hers. She nodded at Meenakshi in the manner of one who had been introduced to her before, which filled Meenakshi with immediate dread.

'You don't remember me at all, do you?' said the young woman, who appeared to be two or three years older than Meenakshi.

'Should I?'

'My name's Kala.' When Meenakshi didn't respond with immediate comprehension, she went on, 'I studied at the Academy for three years? The non-magical curriculum. We met once at a History exam?'

'Oh.' Meenakshi made a wild stab. 'You were the one with fourteen pages of notes on the Battle of the Eight Djinn!'

'Yes,' said Kala, looking pleased. 'Of course, after all that, it didn't come up in the exam. Do you know anything about the first test?' The field itself was still shrouded in magical mist, to hide the test from spectators and contestants alike until Vasundhara announced it. 'I heard it's archery.'

༄

Nalini, Kamakshi and Persis stood around a table, on which were spread all the readouts that had been supplied by the Sprites. Slips of paper squiggled across the wooden surface and spilled onto the floor.

'We can Summon him back,' said Kamakshi.

'We're *not* going to try it,' Nalini said firmly. 'If we can't successfully overcome the existing Summons, we'll kill him. *That'll* be trouble.'

'Then we have no plan,' said Kamakshi. 'We've spent hours and hours looking at these fiddly bits of paper that tell us absolutely nothing. So have the Sprites. It's not hard to Summon a Sprite, and it could have been done from *anywhere.*'

'If we'd found the room sooner,' Nalini said, 'we might have been able to trace the residual magic to its source. If only that thrice-cursed Das hadn't been more worried about his reputation than the damage he might to do Inter-Realm relations . . . '

'Never mind the thrice-cursed Das,' said Persis. 'I don't object to turning him into the four-times-cursed Das, but that can wait until after we've found the Sprite. We must think of *something.*' She gestured impatiently. The scraps of paper flew off the table and piled themselves into an untidy heap in the corner. 'There. *That's* out of the way. Forget the readouts and start at the beginning. Someone Summoned the Sprite. How do we find out who it was?'

'If they still have him—which they must, or he would have come to the swayamvara or sent word in some way—then it can't be easy to hold him. Nobody keeps a Summoned Sprite for *this* long—a few hours at most. They'll need a magician on it, *all* the time.'

'That doesn't help us when he could have been Summoned from anywhere in the world,' Kamakshi said gloomily.

'What about the ransom note?' Persis asked. 'How was that delivered?'

'Left outside Vasundhara's door. That's no good. With portals regulations relaxed for the swayamvara, there have been far too many strangers coming and going—especially in the palace. There's no way we'll be able to narrow it down.'

'There'll be another one,' Persis said. 'With instructions on how to exchange the Fire of the East for the Sprite.'

'It probably won't be delivered the same way.'

'It'll be delivered *somehow*. We should stop running all over the city looking for clues—now that we know the Sprite was Summoned. He could be anywhere. It's a waste of time. We can get some people watching Vasundhara and the palace.'

'That's easily arranged,' Nalini said, going to the door. 'I'll do it now.'

♪

' . . . and our delight is greater than my simple words can express. It is a sign of the international goodwill we all strive towards that people from around the world, and beyond it, have honoured our invitation to this momentous occasion.'

Kalban sighed. He had a high tolerance for speeches, but even he was growing weary. It felt like the Maharaja had been droning on for days.

'Now I have only one more thing to say,' boomed the magically enhanced voice.

'Do you think he *means* it this time?' said Abhinav.

Kalban had no idea why he had been placed next to Abhinav when, for the most part, delegations from different places had been thoroughly mixed, ostensibly to allow people to make friends. It had probably been Vasundhara's idea of a joke.

'This is the longest speech I've ever heard him make,' Kalban said. 'But he *does* seem to be getting to the end of his scroll.'

Sure enough, a few minutes later, the Maharaja concluded by wishing all competitors the best of luck, expressing a hope that the most suitable candidate would win while assuring everyone than no imputation of *unsuitability* was being made about the losers, and ceding the podium to Vasundhara to explain the test.

The competitors, standing in a semicircle around the base of the podium, became suddenly more attentive. The two from Melucha were listening harder than all the rest. For a moment, Kalban felt sorry for them. Even if Ravi *hadn't* been in the picture, they wouldn't have had a chance.

There was a sudden commotion.

Heads turned around the field as, just in time to avoid being considered heinously discourteous, one final guest arrived, sweeping through the gate and straight to Vasundhara.

She was a woman, if a being made of light and air might be called a woman. She was beautiful, if so mundane a word might be used to describe her otherworldly loveliness.

She was more dangerous than any of the archers, the guards, or, for that matter, most of the magicians gathered.

Having clasped Vasundhara's hands warmly, the woman looked around. Half a dozen ushers materialized to take her to her place, beside the Master Sorcerer.

'Oh *no*,' Kalban hissed under his breath. 'Oh no, no, *no* . . . Not *there*.'

'Why?' asked Abhinav. 'Who is she?'

'Rambha,' Kalban said grimly. 'The Chief of the Celestial Dancers. And you can *bet* she's going to spend the whole time pumping the Master Sorcerer for information about how we're trying to recover the Sprite.'

'What does it matter if she does?'

Kalban, in the shock of the moment, almost told him. Then he shook his head. 'At least, Asamanjas is there. And the Maharani. Where's Meenakshi?'

'There, next to the Yaunic Ambassador,' Abhinav said, pointing. '*He* looks like he's pumping her for information. They've been talking since he arrived.'

'Never mind the Yaunic Ambassador.' Kalban crossed his arms and stared at the field. He wasn't *doing* anything he shouldn't— so far he'd only looked at Amsuman's will, and that was no crime. He wasn't even *planning* to lay hands on the—

He willed himself not to think about it. It was rumoured that Rambha could read minds. Although Paras and Nalini had both, separately, assured him that it was untrue, he didn't want to take the chance.

He would be conspicuous if he left, so he had no choice but to sit there and try to keep his attention on the competition. The magical mist covering the field had been lifted to reveal the complex test Vasundhara had devised. Kalban wasn't quite sure what the archers were meant to do, but it seemed to involve horses and a great many magical distractions in the form of Illusions and flashing lights.

The first mounted archer was taking his place at the starting line. The targets around the tower were moving in uneven loops. Several people behind them were whispering about the wind. The pleasant breeze blowing over the rest of the field had intensified into what amounted to a gale around the middle.

Kalban had never been fond of archery, but he was prepared to be its most ardent, if not its most informed, admirer for the rest of the morning.

He glanced at Rambha, and then turned his attention firmly to the targets, swaying dangerously as they were buffeted by the wind.

'You must have known she was invited,' Abhinav said.

'She's always invited to major events in Pür and Khand. She almost never comes. She sends a deputy. Don't talk. She's looking at us.'

'She's looking in this general direction. There are hundreds of people.'

A collective, satisfied groan from the assembled crowd indicated that the first archer's performance had been below par. The second archer came on to a cacophony of cheers. He must be local.

Despite himself, Kalban was watching Rambha rather than the archery. He saw the woman, not one of the palace staff, who slipped through the crowd with a silver salver, which she deposited on a table between Rambha and Paras. Neither of them noticed it at first.

There was a thud, a clatter, and scattered laughter as one horse, deciding it wanted nothing to do with towers that shook and rattled for no discernible reason, deposited its rider in a heap on the grass and trotted away towards the gate.

The fifth contestant was on the field before Rambha, chancing to glance down, saw the salver and snatched up what seemed to be a letter.

She opened it.

Her brows came down.

CHAPTER VIII

'You have to admire the audacity of it,' Kamakshi said, 'whoever it was.'

'*Audacity?*' Asamanjas groaned. 'Trouble, that's what you mean. Trouble for us—trouble for everyone. This is,' he went on, voice rising in pitch, 'an unmitigated disaster.'

'You really should retire,' Nalini said. Her voice oozed sympathy. 'All this stress *can't* be good for you. Just think of the strain on your heart.'

'Never mind the strain on my heart. What I want you—*all* of you,' he went on in a stronger tone, his glare encompassing his brother, Nalini, Kamakshi, Persis, Meenakshi and Kalban, 'to tell me is what we're going to do when this goes *wrong* and Rambha is out for blood.'

'Blame the Maharaja,' suggested Paras. 'The man's always whinging at me about how he's *responsible* for what I do and that's why I need to tell him when I begin a new experiment. Let him *be* responsible for once.'

'Paras isn't wrong,' said Nalini. 'The Maharaja knows what's happening.'

'That won't fly with Rambha. She doesn't care about mortal politics. As far as she's concerned, responsibility ends with the Master Sorcerer. And if she finds out about Meenakshi—'

'Meenakshi's underage. We talked about this.'

'We did, and that was fine before *this* happened.'

As one, everyone looked at the single sheet of paper on the table.

The paper on the silver salver had turned out to be not, as Kalban had hoped in the first desperate instant, a letter from a secret admirer, such as Celestial Dancers were wont to receive by the dozen. It had been a note from Ravi's kidnapper.

I hope you're searching, the note said. *You have five days. I'll let you know how to contact me when you've found the Fire of the East.*

Rambha, upon reading it, had made her excuses to the Maharaja and asked to speak to Nalini and Paras. She had been politely (Rambha was always exquisitely polite, until the moment when someone made her angry) but firmly insistent that nobody was to find, look for, discuss or even *consider* recovering the Fire of the East.

'It's gone,' Rambha had said, 'hopefully lost in the bowels of the earth, and good *riddance*. It brought nothing but trouble. If the little idiot has managed to get himself kidnapped—'

'He could hardly avoid being Summoned,' Nalini had murmured.

'He could avoid, and *should* have avoided, being put in a position where someone would Summon him in order to hold him for ransom. Sprites and Dancers are forbidden mortal entanglements for precisely this reason. Do your best to recover him—I'll be grateful if you do—but *not* at the cost of giving some unhinged psychopath the Fire of the East . . . Oh, and I trust I'll be kept informed if the kidnapper sends another message?'

Asamanjas, on hearing an abbreviated account of events from Paras, had called an immediate meeting.

'What are you suggesting we do?' said Nalini.

'Stop looking for the Fire of the East! Now that Rambha's got this note, she'll be breathing down our necks.'

'I think,' Persis said, 'there's a more important question—*why* did Rambha get the note? If the kidnapper really *wants* the Fire of the East . . . this was counterproductive. Did anyone see who delivered the note?'

'I did,' said Kalban. 'It was a woman—nobody I know.'

'That's helpful,' said Nalini.

'Maybe it *is* helpful,' Kamakshi said. 'It *would* have been audacious to deliver the ransom note to Rambha herself—but maybe it was an accident. Rambha was dripping with gold. She was sitting next to the Maharani. Maybe the note was meant for Vasundhara.'

'That can't be,' said Paras. 'Everyone knows Vasundhara. *And* Rambha.'

'Everyone in *Pür* knows Vasundhara,' Persis said. 'And might be expected, in any case, to be able to tell the difference between a human woman and the Chief of the Celestial Dancers. Someone who had never seen either of them—and who only saw Rambha from behind, sitting in a place of honour, as bejewelled as a bride—someone like that *might* make a mistake.'

'The kidnapper's from outside Pür?' Asamanjas said hopefully.

'Not necessarily. It might have been a ploy to avoid being recognized—the woman who delivered the letter might not be the kidnapper. But it's a place to start. Kalban, would you know her if you saw her again?'

'Yes, but how are we going to find her?'

'Scry the crowd,' Nalini said, getting to her feet. 'There's an hour of the competition left. She might still be there . . . but, no, that's no good. There'll be too many people.'

'We can interview the staff,' Persis said. 'Someone might have noticed her.'

'Good, I'll leave that to you,' said Asamanjas. 'So we're giving up looking for the Fire of the East, then?' Everyone turned to him, Meenakshi and Paras in particular looking scandalized, and the others mildly disapproving. 'What?'

'We can't *give up*,' Meenakshi said. 'What if we *don't* find whoever delivered the message?'

'Rambha might *say* it's not worth the risk,' Nalini said, 'but she's a Celestial Dancer, and it's a Sprite who's missing. Whether or not she admits it to herself, she *will* have trouble if he's not returned in one piece. Trouble for Rambha means trouble for us. We need to find the Fire of the East.'

'I hate to admit it,' Chitralekha said, 'but the Head of the Inter-Realm Liaison Bureau wasn't *wrong*. There's always been tension between us and the Sprites. They keep complaining that they don't have as many inborn safeguards in the Mortal Realm as Celestial Dancers do—'

'A complaint that present events seem to justify,' Kalban commented.

'There are no safeguards against being Summoned. The Inter-Realm Accord does have a clause to protect immortal beings who live in the Mortal Realm for an extended period—'

'Really?' said Meenakshi. 'I've never seen it.'

'It's in one of the Appendices. The Inter-Realm Ambassador in Pür maintains a full list. It's meant to protect the Embassy staff and any others who are put in place to watch over events—as Mada was last year,' she added, twinkling at Kalban.

'And you're not going to tell me who's replaced him, I suppose.'

'That would defeat the purpose. Regardless, if Ravi ends up dead, the Sprites *will* make trouble—for Rambha, certainly, and for Pür if they feel like the Maharaja's attempts to recover him were . . . too weak. There's talk in the Inter-Realm that the Sprites are preparing to act against the kidnapper if Ravi isn't found safely.'

'That would lead to war.'

'That's why we *must* find the Fire of the East.'

'We're up against a dead end!' said Kalban in frustration. 'All we have are some vague, five-hundred-year-old directions from Amsuman's will. We can't be the first to have found *those*, so I'm sure it's not as easy as digging up a treasure chest.'

'The instructions are a start.' Meenakshi spread a map on the table. 'I found this in an old atlas in the library downstairs. I've copied and enlarged it. It's a map of the northern parts of Pür at the time Rajgir was built.'

The map showed few contours around the city, which was unsurprising. The site of Rajgir had been chosen for its flatness.

The Tatini, which began as a glacial stream in the mountains north of Rajgir, was marked out in blue, flowing in its present course. Patches of green marked stands of long-dead trees.

'*Beginning from Rajgir, the foundation stone I laid,*' Chitralekha read from the copy Kalban had made of the will, '*walk west for four days so that you find yourself in the midst of the desert.*'

'*Walk west for four days?*' Meenakshi muttered. 'That's a vague way to give directions. No bearings, no measurable distances . . . No *wonder* nobody's found the Fire of the East yet.'

'The magicians of Amsuman's time hadn't discovered how to open Mortal Realm portals,' Chitralekha reminded her. 'They had to walk—or ride, I suppose—everywhere.'

'They might not have discovered portals, but I *know* they'd invented comprehensible units of distance. I assume he means the Kos Desert. It's here . . . ' Meenakshi indicated a large swathe of yellow on the map. 'And we just have to assume he could be referring to any part of it because we have no idea how quickly he walked.'

'*There you will see the famed statue of the Goddess of Speech, guardian of unruly tongues. It stands as tall as five men.*' Chitralekha looked up. 'Does either of you know which statue he means?'

'No. It might not even exist any more. If the sand covered it . . . '

'Right, let's go on. *A great tunnel runs under the statue. To enter it, you must ask a magician's aid. Go north in the tunnel. You must walk for three days. At the end of it lies what remains of the treasure of Tara the Starchaser.*'

'This is useless,' said Kalban. 'We'll just end up wandering in circles in the desert. Why he couldn't choose a better place to hide his treasure . . . '

Meenakshi was bent over the map. 'Wouldn't going north for three days take you out of the desert?'

'Listen to the rest. *And though it be easy to find the place where the treasure is hidden, it shall not be easy to take it, for it is guarded by a mighty guardian.*'

'A mighty guardian must mean an *immortal* guardian?' Kalban noted. 'Can you find out?'

'Not without Rambha's hearing about it.'

'There must be legends!' Meenakshi looked up. 'Oh, maybe not something as well known as the phoenix on the Mountain of Ice, but local stories—*something*. If there *has* been an immortal guardian for five hundred years—you *know* no immortal being is going to sit around idle doing nothing. There *must* be a place people don't go—where horses throw their shoes and people sprain their ankles and carts break their axles.'

Kalban sighed. 'I suppose I'm going to the minstrels again, not that they were helpful last time.'

'I'll come with you,' Meenakshi said. 'I need to find Vasundhara. I promised to help her set up for this afternoon.'

'What's this afternoon?'

'Philosophy,' said Meenakshi. 'She wanted something a little less strenuous after this morning.'

'That's a logical thing to test,' Chitralekha said. 'The consort has to sit through *hours* of scholarly debates in court . . . especially when, like Princess Vasundhara, the monarch doesn't have the patience for it. What do *you* need to do? Surely a debate doesn't require magical preparation.'

'Oh—she needed a little help with some Alchemy. I'll be back soon.'

Forestalling any questions, Meenakshi opened a portal to the palace and was gone.

'Before you go after her,' came Gopali's voice from the door, 'is it true that you saw the woman who delivered the note to Rambha?'

'You *know* about that?' said Kalban. It was astonishing how Gopali managed to hear things that had nothing to do with her.

'Nalini and your mother have been speaking to all the palace staff. So, of course, they're talking to each other.' Gopali wrinkled her nose. 'I've never known such a place for gossip.'

'That surprises you?' said Chitralekha, 'In all my centuries of visiting the Mortal Realm, I've never known so many people from so many different nations gathered together as are here now, for the swayamvara of Princess Vasundhara. I'm not surprised there's gossip. I'm not even surprised Ravi was taken. I just hope that's the *worst* that happens.'

'Never mind that. Kalban, *is* it true that you saw her? Would you recognize her?'

'Yes, why? Did *you* see her?'

'The staff are denying any involvement, even the most innocent. Nobody was given a note for Rambha. Nobody knows *anything* at all about what's happening. We have to account for the possibility,' Gopali added, 'that the fear that admitting to any knowledge might lead to an interview with the Master Sorcerer might be making them dissemble.'

'That would be no reason to lie,' Kalban argued. 'Paras won't hold it against anyone that they passed on a note without making enquiries.'

'You know that. I know that. Persis and Nalini and Kamakshi know that. The average citizen of Rajgir *doesn't* know it. Saha and I might have seen her—I noticed a woman carrying a tray. She *wasn't* dressed like one of the palace staff. That's why she stood out.'

'I saw that, but clothes are easy to change. It might have been anyone,' said Kalban. 'Vraja have brought their own staff and crocodile handlers—and Khand has taken up half the inns in the city.'

'The woman I saw was entering the top seating area. I noticed because I thought she must have something to do with the test.'

'You *saw* her?'

'I saw where she went afterwards. To the seating area on the right—where the courtiers and lords and ladies from Rajgir were seated.'

'Did she speak to anyone?'

'I didn't notice—how was I to know?' Gopali protested, when Kalban looked disapproving. 'I told you, I thought she was taking something to Vasundhara for the test. I had no idea she was a suspicious character. Why didn't *you* take note of where she went? You *saw* her make a delivery to Rambha.'

'I was too busy watching Rambha.'

'At least we know where to start looking.'

'In the noble and lordly households of Rajgir? That's going to be easy. They only employ thousands of people among them.'

CHAPTER IX

The Maharaja stood at the top of the tiers of seats, watching the preparations with mingled pride and anxiety. It was *something* to have a granddaughter who could face her swayamvara with grace, not letting the non-appearance of her favoured suitor deter her from ensuring that those remaining would face as stiff a test as the honour of Pür demanded.

It was something else entirely when that test required the involvement of the young lady who would probably be Master Sorcerer one day.

The Maharaja of Pür had nothing against magic. He depended on it to keep his kingdom running smoothly and prevent famines and plagues and other things that led to a discontented populace. He *liked* magic.

It was just that he liked it best when it was being practiced in a different part of the kingdom by someone whose skill extended no further than making pretty fireworks.

'Are you *certain* it needs to be quite so . . . vigorous?' he asked.

The acoustics of the hall were excellent. His voice carried, without losing a decibel of disapproval, to the centre of the well, where Meenakshi was kneeling at the edge of what the Maharaja suspected to be a superfluous mandala she had chalked out on the floor.

Meenakshi shrugged. 'I thought that was the point.'

'Of course that's the point,' Vasundhara said briskly. The Maharaja suspected that Meenakshi would cause far fewer surprises if people like his granddaughter didn't *abet* her every chance they got. 'It's not a *test* otherwise.'

'It might frighten people,' said the Maharaja.

Because standing at the top of the steps and bellowing into the well of the hall was making no impression on his audience, he made his way down to them. He might as well save his lungs for when they might have a real effect.

Green flames shot up as the Maharaja crossed the lines of the mandala. Something snarled inside them.

He scowled.

'It's just an Illusion,' said Meenakshi, unperturbed.

'It's an Illusion that has too many teeth and claws,' said the Maharaja.

'I would call it just the right number. It matches the picture exactly,' Vasundhara said happily, waving a book at her grandfather. 'Perhaps it could have done with a spiked tail—'

'*No* spiked tail,' said the Maharaja, before Meenakshi could put the suggestion into effect. 'What, exactly, is this *thing* going to do?'

'It's an *Illusion*,' Meenakshi said. 'It can't *do* anything.' She got to her feet, dusting off her hands. 'It'll last until dawn. So you can split them into groups, which I assume is the intention?'

'Yes,' Vasundhara says. 'What happens if one of them accidentally touches it or tries to erase the chalk?'

'If they erase the chalk, nothing. It's just there for decoration. If they touch it, they might feel a slight tingle.'

'Wonderful,' muttered the Maharaja. 'Something more for them to file complaints about.'

'Something *more*?' asked Meenakshi. 'Have they filed complaints already about something? This morning was just a standard archery test.'

'And somehow Vraja, consistent producer of the finest archers of the Free Lands, had both its competitors come in last. They're insisting that we cheated.'

'Oh. *Did* you cheat?'

'It's my swayamvara,' Vasundhara said, 'not an international sporting competition. It's only cheating if I say it's cheating.'

'This is going to end in war,' the Maharaja said. 'Just wait and see.'

'Speaking of seeing,' said Vasundhara, 'hadn't you better see about your wardrobe for this evening? Your dressmaker was looking for you about some damask you ordered. The shipment's been delayed.'

'What?' yelped the Maharaja. 'Then I'll have to have brocade *again*. When reports go back to Khand and Yauna, they're going to call us unfashionable provincials.' He rushed off, everything about his demeanour suggesting a man about to harangue his tailor.

Vasundhara smiled a satisfied smile. 'That'll keep him occupied until it's time to begin the debate. I wanted to speak to you alone. How's it going with the search? Are you likely to find the gem in time?'

'I don't know. Maybe. We need—Kalban was going to ask the minstrels, but maybe *you* know. It *might* be hidden somewhere north of the Kos Desert—is there a statue of the Goddess of Speech in the desert? A giant one? It would be hundreds of years old.'

'Not that I know.'

'All right. Second option. Somewhere that would be about three days' walk—whatever *that* means—north of this statue—'

'So *not* in the desert any more.'

'And the place is guarded by . . . some sort of immortal being. There must be stories.'

'Far too many. In the north of Pür, every village tells of a dozen or more forest and river deities, not to speak of vengeful spirits. There's no way you can investigate them all in less than a week. Meenakshi, you *have* to find it.'

'I know, you want Ravi back alive—'

'I *need* him back alive. I *want* to marry him, but my first duty is to the country and it'll be war if we don't find him . . . a devastating war. The Sprites will rebel against Rambha and Urvashi. The Djinn and Yakshas might join them. Nalini thinks so. The Inter-Realm Accord will be as good as dead. Meenakshi, if it comes to that—we'll have to comply with the ransom demand.'

'We *can't* give anyone the Fire of the East,' Meenakshi said. 'And you're not thinking objectively.'

'You know Nalini will do it.'

'She won't. She just wants it for leverage.'

'That's ridiculous. Why would she need it for leverage if she didn't actually intend, in the final extreme, to *give* it to the kidnapper? Nalini may not care whom I marry, but she does care about maintaining Inter-Realm relations—and Rambha may be the strongest and most ancient of the Celestial Dancers, but she's a *fool* if she thinks she'll be able to control the Sprites if she decides to sit about doing nothing while one of their own is killed.'

'I'll make sure I don't give it to Nalini.'

'Meenakshi!' For a moment Vasundhara looked as though she was about to start shouting. Then, with a sigh, she said, 'All right, I know you tend to look at things in black and white. You're far from stupid. If we use the stone to get Ravi back—'

'You mean give a powerful magical artefact to a deranged kidnapper—'

'Then we have *one* potential threat to deal with. If Ravi is killed, we could be facing far worse. Just *think* about it. That's all I ask . . . How do you get on with Abhinav?'

'Who?' Meenakshi asked, startled by the unexpected change of subject.

'Kalban's brother. Abhinav. Does he infuriate you enough for you to turn him into a tortoise?'

'Oh. *Abhinav.*' Meenakshi considered. 'I . . . I don't think so? I've not turned him into a tortoise yet. I haven't seen much of him here,' she added fairly. 'In Melucha, I had Kalban breathing down my neck about the magic laws.'

'Oh.' Vasundhara shrugged. 'Oh, well. It's a swayamvara. It needs *some* excitement.'

'You're *asking* me to turn him into a tortoise?'

'I'm going to put you next to him this evening . . . yes, I know,' she said, when Meenakshi made a face. 'I hadn't planned it. After this morning, Vraja and Khand aren't on speaking terms so we've had to do some rearranging. It's either Abhinav or one of the nobles from Khand. The choice is yours.'

'Abhinav,' Meenakshi decided. 'But I'm not going to make small talk with him, I warn you now. Isn't it time you were getting dressed?'

'You're right,' Vasundhara said gloomily. 'It is.'

✦

Kalban was about to open a portal and go after Meenakshi when there was hard rapping on the door.

'What?' he snapped.

The door opened. One of Asamanjas's aides waved a note at Kalban. 'You. I was told you'd be here. Hurry up. You're wanted.'

Kalban suppressed a sigh. Prince-heir of Melucha he might be, and a fully licensed magician, but Asamanjas's aides still thought of him as a lowly apprentice who could be addressed as *You, hurry up*.

'Wanted by whom?'

'Someone from Melucha came here looking for you. Woman by the name of Rati. She's waiting in the antechamber downstairs. Lord Asamanjas is anxious about her waiting in the antechamber downstairs, so let's sort this out quickly, yes?'

'What does she want?'

'She said she wanted *you*. Hurry *up*.'

'Go,' said Chitralekha. 'The sooner you deal with her, the sooner you can go find out if there are any likely-sounding treasure guardian spirits.'

Kalban left the room. Asamanjas's aide followed him.

'I *know* where the antechamber is,' Kalban said irritably.

'And you also know how to get lost on your way there. I've not forgotten the incident with the ambassador from Khand.'

'That was years ago!' Kalban paused outside the door to the antechamber. 'All right, I'm here. You can go now.'

'I'll be waiting just outside to help escort your friend off the premises.'

'She's not my friend. She doesn't even like me. Isn't Madh normally more hospitable than this?'

'The Master of the Royal Academy is arriving tonight,' said Asamanjas's aide, and his voice couldn't have been more dire if he had been announcing that Yauna had just sent a declaration of war.

Kalban stared at him. When he was in a charitable mood, Paras referred to the Master of the Royal Academy as *that charlatan*.

'He never attends these things!'

'Rambha *requested* that all Licensed magic users powerful enough to be on the watchlist to come to Rajgir. She wants to keep her eye on them . . . and as I'm sure you can imagine, the Head of the Inter-Realm Liaison Bureau thought it best to oblige her. The Master of the Royal Academy didn't *want* to come, but the Master Sorcerer is his superior, so . . . '

'Who's going to keep the peace?'

'Lord Asamanjas is, and that's why he wants all outsiders, *especially* non-magical outsiders, *off the premises*.' After a moment's pause, he added, 'I don't suppose Lord Asamanjas meant you. You can stay.'

'How *kind*.'

Then Kalban went to see Rati.

Although Rati was trying to appear in control of the situation, it pleased Kalban to see that she wasn't entirely succeeding. Her hands were clasped in her lap, firmly, as though she wanted to avoid touching the air.

Kalban knew better than to gloat.

'May I help you?' he said politely.

'Have you considered,' said Rati, 'that you would do better as ambassador to Pür, or even Madh, than as Prince Regnant of Melucha? You appear to better advantage here.'

'Is that why you're here?'

'No. I know a Sprite's been kidnapped. I know your mother is helping in the search for him—and I support that,' Rati added grudgingly. 'She's a powerful magician and Melucha should be seen as playing its part in maintaining Inter-Realm relations. I want to know what *you're* doing.'

'I take it you asked my mother—'

'And her friends Nalini and Kamakshi. I liked them both. They were exceedingly courteous and not at all helpful.'

'Then you should know I can't help you, either. I *am* a licensed magician.'

'All the more reason why you should make good decisions in the matter of engaging in illegal activities.'

'What makes you think there's anything illegal happening?'

'I'm not a fool. I saw Rambha this morning. I know something happened. I *know* Meenakshi is involved—'

'Meenakshi was at the archery contest.'

'She was. Let me tell you what I deduce from that. Other than the Master Sorcerer and Meenakshi, no powerful magician from Madh or any other part of Pür was at the archery contest. The Master Sorcerer is also the Governor of the Southern Provinces of Pür, and couldn't miss such an important event. But if his *wife* could, having come all the way from the Eastern Isles to attend the swayamvara, miss it in order to search for the missing Sprite, I'm certain his daughter could as well.'

'What does any of this have to do with me?'

'In a matter of such importance—and I *do* agree that it's important to find the Sprite—I would expect that the young lady who is widely regarded as the most powerful magician of her generation to be part of the search. If, instead, she is clearly visible talking to the Yaunic Ambassador, I can only assume that the intention *was* that she should be seen . . . and since Rambha was there, I assume it was for Rambha's benefit. Tell me I'm wrong.'

Kalban crossed his arms and glared.

'Very well then,' said Rati. 'If Meenakshi's involved in something, it seems reasonable to suppose that you are, too.'

'I thought you trusted Meenakshi.'

'I do. And it's clear that several people, including your mother, know what she's doing, so it can't be a *secret* plot, whatever else it is. But magicians tend to get a little *too* involved in what they do to see what's really happening. Meenakshi is young. So are you.'

'What difference does that make?'

'I came here because this seems to be the only place to catch you—to warn you to be sensible. I'll be frank. If the worst consequence of all this is that you disgrace yourself and get called up by the Inter-Realm Magical Council, I won't be heartbroken. But trouble for you means trouble for Melucha. I don't want that.'

'Thank you. I'll be careful.'

'Good. And now you're going to say goodbye to that man outside, and you're going to come with me to *our* embassy and tell me everything—'

'You're confident, for someone talking to a magician in the High Commission of Madh.'

'Oh, please,' said Rati. 'We both know you're not nearly as sinister as you're trying to pretend. I'm confident because I have leverage. If you don't tell me what's happening, I'm going straight to Rambha to tell her that you're doing something you don't want her to know about.'

'You would put the Inter-Realm Accord at risk because you don't want to be left out of a secret that has nothing to do with you?'

Rati said nothing.

Kalban considered her in silence. There was no knowing if it was an empty threat. Of course, here, on the territory of Madh, it didn't matter. He could leave the room and ask for the senior-most member of the Inter-Realm Liaison Bureau on the premises, and let them handle it.

He took a step towards the door.

He paused. The Inter-Realm Liaison Bureau *was* known for diplomacy; on the other hand, the magicians of Madh were known for being unable to understand that other countries had *laws* about the practice of magic.

There might be some advantage in telling Rati a part of the truth.

Meenakshi settled into her seat, thinking with some complacency that at least she didn't have to try to be *polite*. If she offended Abhinav, Kalban could deal with it.

For the moment she was alone. At the Maharani's insistence, she had come early and would stay until the end of the debate, to ensure that nothing went wrong with the Illusion. She had explained, and Vasundhara had explained, that nothing *could* go wrong: an Illusion couldn't interact with the physical world.

There was no point arguing with the Maharani. Kings, queens, tyrants and despots had tried, persevered and given up. Meenakshi did not waste energy in a lost cause.

At least, she wasn't in the first row. And she had a book.

She was happily occupied with the latest treatise from one of her favourite Yaunic philosophers when a cleared throat cut into her thoughts. She looked up.

The room was more than half full. Every single person in it was staring at the creature in the middle of the well. Abhinav had arrived and was standing beside his chair, which he held with a white-knuckled grip.

'What is *that*?' he said.

'Don't worry. It's just a distraction for the debaters.'

'It has eight rows of teeth.'

'Ten,' Meenakshi corrected.

'*You* did this?' Abhinav turned to look at her in much the same manner as the High Priest of the Sun God usually did, as though trying to decide if Meenakshi was a troublemaker or simply insane.

Accustomed as she was to the expression, Meenakshi didn't let it worry her.

'A fine bit of Illusion,' she told Abhinav, 'even if I do say so myself. I'm especially pleased with the screaming. That's based on the griffons. They're gentler than kittens, but you wouldn't know it from the noise they make.'

'Gentler than kittens.' Abhinav sat. Carefully, on the edge of his seat, poised to get up and fly if it seemed warranted. 'I should have stayed in Melucha.'

Meenakshi went back to her book.

'*Modern Theories of the Nature of Reality*?' Abhinav asked, looking at the title. 'I'm surprised you're not researching something about the Sprite.' Meenakshi looked up sharply. Whatever was in her face, it made Abhinav recoil. 'I'm just making conversation.'

'What has Kalban told you?'

'*Me*, nothing at all. He told Rati just enough to keep her quiet because she threatened to go to Rambha if he didn't.'

Meenakshi grunted and went back to her book.

'Do you know why people in Melucha don't trust magicians?' Abhinav asked.

'Do I care?'

'It's because magicians get secretive . . . in fairness, everyone gets secretive in Melucha. When *magicians* get secretive, bad things happen.'

'The fact that *you're* not privy to what's happening doesn't mean anybody's being secretive. It's nothing to do with you, anyway.'

'Believe me, I'm glad it isn't. May I offer you some advice?'

'You're *just* like Kalban. Does the need to give advice run in the family?'

'If you don't want Rambha to find out what you're doing—I'm assuming that's why you're sitting here with a book of philosophy—you need someone non-magical to help you. The Dancers don't even know I exist.'

Meenakshi looked up to answer—and her eyes widened as she saw who was in the crowd.

'What is it?' Abhinav asked, alarmed.

'Sprites,' Meenakshi hissed. 'Dozens of them. They weren't expected—where's Vasundhara?'

Almost before she had finished asking the question, Vasundhara was there. She dropped into the empty chair on Abhinav's other side and leaned across him to speak to Meenakshi.

'We couldn't prevent them from entering without causing an incident. Will it affect your magic?'

'The spell will be fine. I was expecting Rambha anyway. I included the standard modifications in anticipation of interference with the magical field. What are they *doing* here?'

'They're armed. They're making a show of force,' Vasundhara said. 'To Rambha as much as to us. We have to get him back, Meenakshi. The Sprites are just *waiting* for an excuse to overthrow Rambha and Urvashi. I'd much rather we didn't give them one on our soil.'

CHAPTER X

'We're running out of time.' Nalini looked around the small room into which everyone was uncomfortably crammed. Paras was at dinner with the Master of the Royal Academy, Rambha and the Maharaja. Since Rambha was so obviously suspicious of them, Nalini had judged it best to avoid the larger chambers that had more potential for listeners-in. 'We have four days left. Unfortunately, knowing that the subject was Summoned makes it difficult for us to find him. Urvashi has a team of Dancers and Sprites reviewing all magical activity around the time he disappeared, but they won't find anything. Most second-year students can Summon a Sprite.'

'An accurate, if unhelpful, summary,' sniped Asamanjas. 'Do you expect me to believe that with nearly all the most powerful magicians of Pür present in Rajgir, we can't recover one Sprite?'

'Not until we know where to look. For all we know, he could have been Summoned to an uninhabited island or a lonely mountaintop. If you want to make yourself *useful* instead of complaining, you can go to the Master of the Royal Academy and tell him to make enquiries among his staff and students.'

'Why me?'

'Because after all that unpleasantness last year, he doesn't like any of the rest of us. He's here, against everybody's wishes. He might as well do *something*. Meenakshi, have you found anything?'

'The Fire of the East might have been part of Amsuman's treasure—'

'The founder of Rajgir?'

'Yes. There are directions, in his will, to some sort of treasure that he claims is guarded by a supernatural being. They're vague. There's something about a statue of the Goddess of Speech in the Kos Desert, but there are no historical records and the statue must be lost now. We just know that the treasure is somewhere to the north of the desert—'

'To the north of the Kos Desert?' Nalini said sharply.

'Yes, why?'

Nalini turned to Asamanjas. 'Isn't Lord Das's country estate in some wilderness north of the Kos Desert?'

'What makes you think I know the country estate of every minor noble?' Asamanjas snapped.

Nalini looked at him.

He sighed. 'Yes, fine, I do know and it is north of the Kos Desert. How does that help? Lord Das isn't a magician.'

'Lord Das's mansion near Rajgir is a recent acquisition. He funded it with treasure he found on his country estate—*and* he told me there's some rumour about a Yakshini in the forest near his home.'

'*And* the Sprite was staying with him,' Persis said. 'It's too much coincidence.'

'Why would he want the Fire of the East?' Meenakshi protested. 'It's useless to him.'

'As a magical artefact, yes,' said Kalban. 'He can sell it on the black market—or to one of the countries that hasn't signed the Inter-Realm Accord. He would be richer than the Maharaja.'

'That might be enough of an incentive to risk angering Rambha,' acknowledged Nalini.

'He can't have been acting alone,' said Kamakshi. 'Maybe he has motive, but he *couldn't* have Summoned the Sprite. Someone did it for him.'

'He could have hired someone,' said Nalini. 'The Summoning Service is becoming popular. Any magical being that exists, they'll Summon for you. It's an absolute nightmare to regulate, let me tell you—for us *and* for the Dangerous Beings Control Squad.'

'Putting your administrative difficulties aside . . .' began Asamanjas.

'That must be the first time you've ever put administrative difficulties aside,' Nalini said sweetly. 'It's so nice that you're learning new things in your old age.'

'*Putting your administrative difficulties aside*,' growled Asamanjas, 'it might be sensible to go to Lord Das's country estate to look for the Sprite. If he hired someone from the Summoning Service, that would be the perfect location to hold the Sprite . . . and even otherwise, you might find clues.'

'Meenakshi and I are going anyway,' said Kalban. 'We can go and look.'

'No, you don't go anywhere *near* his house or any people,' Nalini said. 'Leave *that* side of things to us. Fortunately, the Portals

Regulation Authority isn't restricting activity within Rajgir—they won't till after the swayamvara is over—'

'You want to go *now*?' Asamanjas asked.

'Maybe—'

'*No*,' Kamakshi said. 'We're not prepared. We can't go in blindly, when we don't know what we might find—and neither can you,' she added to Meenakshi and Kalban. 'The day after tomorrow is a rest day for the swayamvara and the first round of unsuccessful candidates will have been notified. Many of them will go home—'

'With their delegations,' Persis finished. 'Which means there'll be dozens of portals open and a couple more will go under the radar.'

'*And* nobody will be expecting to see us anywhere in particular,' added Nalini. 'It's perfect.'

'You're definitely going with Meenakshi, aren't you?' Persis asked Kalban.

'Of course. Why?'

'A Yakshini who's been bound to the Mortal Realm for hundreds of years isn't a danger anyone should try to face alone, even Meenakshi . . . ' She hesitated. 'Even if we find Ravi, it's still best to recover the Fire of the East. Otherwise, we may end up with another kidnapping and ransom demand next year. Make certain you're fully equipped. It's good that there's an extra day.'

'What if we're wrong about the Fire of the East being there?' Meenakshi asked.

'We're not wrong,' Nalini said with calm certainty. 'I *knew* all along that that thrice-cursed Das was hiding something. And now there's something *we* can do,' she went on. 'We can find out if he hired a magician from the Summoning Service, and if not we can find out who he's been meeting.'

'Summoning Service records are confidential.'

Kamakshi scoffed. 'This is a serious crime.'

'I'm *sure* the manager of the Summoning Service can be induced to see things our way,' Persis said.

'I can't *believe* you told Rati!'

'I knew what I was doing,' said Kalban. 'We would have had to put someone on her every *minute* to keep her from going to Rambha with her suspicions. This way, she's happy, she won't interfere, and she might actually try to *help* us.'

Kalban and Meenakshi were in the small library at the Madh High Commission. It was empty, save the two of them. Several of Rajgir's nobles were hosting parties to commemorate Vasundhara's swayamvara and nearly everyone who *didn't* know what they were doing was at one or the other of them. Nalini, Kamakshi and Asamanjas had gone, each to a different house, in order to hear as much chatter as possible. Kalban's mother had returned to the Embassy of Melucha, promising to make a believable excuse for him.

Not that it would be necessary, since Rati had, to his surprise, accepted the explanation he had given.

'You should have turned her into a frog for a week,' said Meenakshi. 'By then it would all have been over. You were *on* the territory of Madh.'

'The solution to every problem isn't turning people into whatever reptile you fancy that day.'

'Frogs are amphibians.'

Kalban forebore from grinding his teeth. It never helped. 'Never mind Rati,' he said. 'At least, I can control what information I give her.'

'What did you tell her?'

'I told her there's been a ransom demand. I *didn't* tell her we're looking for the stone, though I'm sure she guessed. Rati's not important now.' He gestured at the pile of books in front of Meenakshi. 'What are we looking for?'

'Anything about the Yakshini in the forest near Lord Das's country estate. Your mother's right—a Yakshini who's been bound to the Mortal Realm for hundreds of years is going to be *much* more irritable than one just Summoned, and if it's true that the people who live around have been imagining all sorts of magical powers for her . . . '

'She might have become imbued with some of them?'

'We won't know until we go there.'

Kalban stared at the spines of the books, not really taking in the titles. His years in Madh had inured him to dangers of the magical sort. Rogue Yakshas were an amusing incident, not a serious threat, and even now he didn't harbour any serious doubts that he and Meenakshi between them were capable of handling the Yakshini, extreme irritability and the potential for enhanced powers notwithstanding.

'What are we going to do if we get the Fire of the East?' he said at last.

'Rati asked that, did she?'

'She did. I told her I can't legally lay hands on it.'

'Nalini says we only need it to lure out whoever kidnapped Ravi. Once they show themselves . . . ' Meenakshi shrugged. 'I wouldn't want to be the kidnapper then. Father is unhappy about how much time he's had to spend dining and socializing with Rambha just to prove that he's not on a secret hunt for a contraband artefact.'

Kalban shuddered. The Master Sorcerer hadn't mellowed with age; those who made him unhappy could confidently expect that he would spread the unhappiness in every direction, *particularly* the one it had come from, and with added magical modifications.

There was a commotion outside, heavy boots planting themselves firmly before the door, the sound of an argument. The guards were denying someone entry to the library.

'I told them to make sure nobody interrupted,' Meenakshi said, in response to Kalban's questioning glance.

Kalban nodded.

'Let me pass!' a familiar voice said, its exasperation clear even through the four-inch-thick door. 'I'm the future Maharani of Pür.'

'Standing in the territory of Madh, my lady,' said one of the guards, deferential but firm. Vasundhara might intimidate people, but anyone who had spent any time in the vicinity of magicians knew to be far more worried about them than the future queen.

'Madh is the capital of the Southern Provinces, whose Governor holds his seat at the pleasure of the Maharaja.'

The guard cleared his throat pointedly.

'We won't dispute that now,' Vasundhara conceded. 'I need to speak to Meenakshi. It's urgent. Can you at least call her?'

Kalban went to put the guard out of his misery and let Vasundhara in.

Vasundhara stalked into the room, still dressed in her finery from the state dinner that had followed the debate.

'Tell me you're getting somewhere,' she demanded, sitting down in a jangle of jewellery. 'I left Bahuka almost weeping into his wine, of which, I might add, he's had more in one sitting than he normally consumes in an entire week.'

'Who's Bahuka?' Meenakshi asked, without looking up from her book.

'Oh, *honestly*, Meenakshi! You've met him at least half a dozen times.'

'I've met most of your grandfather's courtiers at least half a dozen times. That's not helpful.'

'He's the Minister for Inter-Realm Affairs—'

'And you're bothering *me* about him? What's Nalini there for? She loves talking to people, and I'm *busy*.'

Vasundhara said nothing. One of her gifts—her greatest gift, according to the Maharani, who had as good an appreciation as anyone for a good seat on a horse and a steady hand on a bow but who *truly* understood how the court worked—was the ability to say nothing when the occasion called for nothing to be said.

This allowed her to gather her thoughts, and to remind herself that it was pointless to expect Meenakshi to care about Bahuka's distress.

'Meenakshi,' she said at last, 'there are dozens of Sprites in Rajgir. They haven't been in the Mortal Realm in these numbers in living memory. They're not here to find Ravi. That's only an

101

excuse. They're here because Rambha is here. There must be many more waiting in the Inter-Realm for Urvashi—'

'If the Sprites are planning a takeover, how is it our business? Especially when nobody's asked for our help?'

'Rambha has a flaw. The same one Urvashi has. Neither of them ever believes they can be overcome, because it's never happened before in all their immortal lives. Maybe if they *had* been mortal and fallible and worried about knives in the back, they would have done better at striking a balance with the Sprites.'

'Still not our business.'

'The Sprites will be far less pleasant to deal with than Rambha and Urvashi, believe me. The Inter-Realm Accord will end and we'll have chaos. Regardless, it isn't interfering to solve a problem that's occurred *in* Rajgir.'

Meenakshi snapped her book shut. 'What, exactly, do you think everyone is trying to *do* here? We have a vague set of directions and we're going to Lord Das's estate based on Nalini's *hunch* and just *hoping* that the Yakshini there is guarding the Fire of the East. Is there anything else you think I should be doing instead?'

The air began to tingle.

Kalban said, warningly, '*Meenakshi.*'

Meenakshi let out a breath. The air cleared.

'Suppose we just leave her to read?' Kalban suggested tactfully.

Vasundhara shook her head. She was a woman of action. She had, as was traditional, served in the army, gaining the respect of grizzled old veterans with her can-do spirit and her unwillingness to back down in the face of danger. It galled and frustrated her that in a matter of such import her role was limited to making sure everything looked normal. That was what consorts were for; that was what Ravi excelled at and why they got on so well together.

'Are you trying to persuade her to give the Fire of the East to the kidnapper?' Kalban said quietly.

Vasundhara's eyes snapped to him. She hadn't realized she'd been *so* transparent.

'It might be the only way to prevent a catastrophe.'

'Vasundhara, this is going to be bad enough as it is when Rambha realizes that we're looking for the thing with the explicit approval of the Master Sorcerer and the Head of the Inter-Realm Liaison Bureau, not to speak of the Maharaja. If a magician gets possession of one of the most powerful magical artefacts known—'

'It can't be worse than all-out war in the Inter-Realm.'

'No? What about all-out war right here in *this* realm?'

Vasundhara sighed. 'Yes, I understand all that. Let's just try to avoid both, shall we?'

'We need to find the Sprite.'

CHAPTER XI

'*S*inging,' Kalban said. '*Really?*'

It was the middle of a sunny morning. Most of the previous night having been devoted to research, it had been judged wisest that he and Meenakshi attend the day's competition. Accordingly, in company with his father and brother, he was making his way down the sloping lawn.

'After yesterday's excitements,' said the Prince Regnant, 'I wonder what the Princess has in store for us. I can't imagine that it's a simple *singing* competition.'

Kalban was about to respond when he felt a prickle of *something*. Magic. Not mortal, and not friendly.

He looked around. It was a minute or two before he spotted the Sprite. He was leaning against a tree, to all outward appearances a guest passing the time until the competition began.

Which was what he *was*, Kalban told himself firmly.

Then the Sprite's lips curved up into a smile, eyes glinting like no mortal's ever did as they met Kalban's.

Kalban stumbled.

'Kalban,' said Shel, 'is everything all right?' The Prince Regnant's voice was as relaxed as ever, but his eyes had sharpened.

Kalban looked back at the tree. The Sprite was striding towards them with grim purpose. His father and brother, following his gaze, stopped and waited.

'I've seen you in Madh,' the Sprite said as soon as he was within earshot. 'The Master Sorcerer's apprentice.'

'I'm not an apprentice any more,' Kalban said.

The Sprite must have known that, but he checked himself. 'A Licensed magician. By the Five Fires, I had best be careful.' Despite his words, his manner lost none of its belligerence. 'Well then, *magician*, what is your *former* master doing to find my friend?' Before Kalban could respond, the Sprite turned to Abhinav. 'You, boy. Do you know where Ravi is?'

'No,' said Abhinav. 'And I suggest you—'

'*No*,' Kalban snapped, stepping in between them to make eye contact with the Sprite. 'Leave us in peace. That's not a request.'

The Sprite glared a moment longer, but he went.

'*Never*,' Kalban said, not taking his eyes off the retreating back, 'never, *never* make a *suggestion* to a being from the Inter-Realm. Give orders or say nothing.'

'I'll remember that,' Abhinav said as they walked on. Kalban was pleased to hear that he sounded shaken.

The tower and archery targets had been removed from the field, which now featured a large raised dais in the centre where the tower had been. The stands were significantly emptier. At a glance, Kalban could see that there was nobody from Vraja other than the two contestants, a bare handful from Khand, and very few of the citizenry of Rajgir.

The Sprites, on the other hand, were increasing in number with each passing moment. And it appeared that a seat was being saved for Rambha.

'It seems that people are afraid,' Kalban's father noted. 'This really *will* end the chances of Vraja's contenders. I doubt they'll have much heart to sing without anyone to cheer them on.'

'I pity those idiots we sent if they somehow end up winning the thing,' said Abhinav.

'Pity the consort of the future Maharani?'

'I pity *anyone* who has to live in Rajgir and deal with magic and all its attendant problems on a regular basis. Nobody's actually entered the contest *expecting* to win it. Everyone thought the Princess would rig it so the Sprite would win.'

'Not Vasundhara,' said Kalban. 'She might *want* to marry Ravi, but if he didn't come out on top on his own merits, she'd have a *lot* to say to him about it.'

'You may not be accurate in your estimate that *nobody* entered the contest expecting to win it,' added Shel, as he nodded his thanks to the attendant who came to show them their seats. 'The two hapless boys *we* sent didn't, that's true, but the others . . .' He paused, looking around in mild curiosity. The edges of the arena had begun to glow. 'Should we be worried?'

'What?' Kalban looked up. 'Oh, that. It's probably just for the acoustics. The Maharaja is particular about acoustics.'

Soon after they were seated, the fanfare began. Then the Maharaja went to the platform to address the gathering.

'I hope this will at least be *quick*,' Kalban's father said.

Kamakshi entered the room where Nalini and Persis were laying out a stock of magical supplies.

'Oh, *not* the emerald protection charms,' she protested, when she saw the handful of green amulets Persis was carefully wrapping in soft cloth. 'They're *fake*. They're not even real emeralds. I told Paras to outlaw them because people were buying them thinking they'd be able to control high-level demons.'

One of the Master Sorcerer's responsibilities was to keep track of and eliminate fake magical aids or books that might put people in danger. Paras, who took this responsibility seriously, could be relied upon to implement strict measures whenever peddlers of mystic baubles, books or elixirs made unverified claims. But even *he* couldn't stem the flow of the illicit trade, which flourished in back alleys and among students at the Academy.

'Diplomatic immunity,' Persis said cheerfully. 'I know they're useless. Let me enjoy myself. In Melucha, I can't wear an amulet where anyone can see it.'

'*Must* you treat this as a game?' said Nalini, sounding pained. 'Have you any *idea* what a time I had with Rambha this morning? Not to speak of the Sprites who have been waylaying me at every corner. A delegation of them nearly came to blows with the Dancers.'

'If you don't like Persis wearing silly jewellery, you're *really* not going to like what I found out. I got the Summoning Service records.'

'Did you have to threaten them?'

'Threaten, coax, point out the most expedient course of action if they didn't want to deal with Paras instead.' Kamakshi shrugged. 'Anyway, I *got* the names of all their customers. They *say* they don't have more than that.'

She held out a list.

Persis and Nalini bent over it.

'Lord Das isn't on it,' said Nalini. 'I didn't seriously expect that he would be. I'm sure he's got more sense than to put his own name to something like this.'

'Never mind Lord Das. Look there.'

Nalini looked at an entry that read *Unnamed*.

'What about it? Lots of people . . . *oh*.' She looked at the address where the service had been delivered. 'The palace? Not the Maharaja or Maharani, surely? Or Vasundhara herself?'

'It may not be,' said Persis. 'Any of the courtiers or palace staff would have access to an empty antechamber.'

'I asked which of the summoners had handled this. It was a freelancer—a man called Rishi and they've not heard from him since then, which isn't unusual. Freelancers show up when they need some extra money and then disappear for months. Payment was in advance.'

'Did you get Rishi's address?'

'What do you take me for?' Kamakshi held up a slip of paper. 'Let's go.'

The Maharaja of Pür wasn't at his best. Although, under duress, he put up with magic, and even appreciated it, he didn't like the idea of Immortals traipsing freely through Rajgir. And yet, at the insistence of the Maharani, he was sitting with the most powerful sorcerer of the Free Lands on one side of him, and the Chief of the Celestial Dancers on the other, and pretending that it didn't set his teeth on edge.

To make matters worse, he couldn't even retreat into happy daydreams of his misspent youth; the Maharani had given him strict instructions to ensure that Paras gave no hint of what Meenakshi was doing.

'Fortunately, we've arranged it so the girl hasn't had time to consult him,' she had said. 'I wouldn't put it past Paras to know anyway. Watch him like a *hawk*.'

'Why tell him at all?' the Maharaja had asked.

The Maharani had looked at him with a pitying smile. 'He's the Master Sorcerer. If this all goes wrong . . . '

Fortunately for the Maharaja, Paras and Rambha had shown no inclination to converse with each other. They looked at each other warily, sidelong, not enemies and not friends.

The tense atmosphere made it impossible for him to pay attention to the singing, which was, he had to admit, all to the good. He couldn't pretend *not* to know why Vasundhara had chosen it as one of the competitions—Sprites generally sang well, and Ravi had a rich, full voice—but, in his absence, it forced the audience to listen to the mediocre vocal abilities of youths who had entered the competition on the strength of either aristocratic pedigrees or martial prowess.

Rambha's mellifluous accents interrupted his thoughts.

'What are you doing to recover the Sprite?'

'Ah,' said the Maharaja. This sort of thing he could answer. 'We are, of course, doing *everything* in our power.'

'Not *you*,' said Rambha, turning a venomous glance on him. The Maharaja recoiled. Who could have thought that such perfection of face and form could look so baleful? 'This entire mess is because of your inability to communicate to your granddaughter the need for discretion and good sense.'

'I really think the Sprite was old enough to—'

'Everyone knows Sprites are witless. Your granddaughter Vasundhara, I've been pleased to note, is a sensible girl. I'm *certain* she would have been reasonable if you had put things to her correctly.'

'But I—'

'I suppose you came down with a heavy hand, and, naturally, the child rebelled. Now there's a Sprite missing in the Mortal Realm.' She turned to Paras, her glare lessening slightly. 'Master Sorcerer, what are you doing about it?'

'Our most talented magicians are searching for the Sprite,' Paras said. 'I have full confidence in their abilities. I know you must be worried—'

'What a thing to suggest! Why, pray, should *I* worry?'

'Have the Sprites come to form your honour guard?'

'Sprites,' Rambha said, with even more contempt than she had just addressed the Maharaja. 'They understand *nothing*. They're impatient and ambitious. They have neither the delicacy nor the wisdom for this difficult task.'

'Are we still speaking about the same thing?' asked the Maharaja.

'I'm sure we *all* understand each other,' Rambha said sweetly.

Rati, accustomed to long and dreary hours of Privy Council meetings, backroom negotiations and listening to reports from sundry double agents, seldom had the freedom to show it when she was bored. She had it now, and exercised it with a feeling of delicious luxury.

'If that's how dull you find it,' Dev said, after her third heavy sigh, 'I don't know why we're even here. The place is teeming with Sprites.'

'The entire *city* is teeming with Sprites. Other parts of it aren't being watched by the Dangerous Beings Control Squad. And the Master Sorcerer. Besides, it would have been even duller at the Embassy. Nobody's there. I see the Yaunic Ambassador is still sitting next to Meenakshi. The man talks enough for ten people! I wonder who persuaded her to put up with it.'

'Why isn't the Tyrant-in-waiting here? Surely the wedding of the Princess of Pür merited his attendance, even if he didn't want to enter the lists himself.'

Rati scoffed. 'The Tyrant-in-waiting is a petulant child who didn't have the courage to come and lose to a Sprite. I don't care about him.' She dropped her voice. 'I came here so I'd have a chance to observe Kalban outside Melucha. He seems a different person.'

'You don't seem happy.'

'I'm not. It's an unnecessary complication. It would have been easier if . . . ' Rati shrugged. 'Never mind. That's not today's problem. Today's problem seems more pressing . . . Oh, look. Meenakshi's got a letter.' She leaned over to Kalban. 'Is that going to be a problem, do you think?'

'What?' asked Kalban, whose eyes were glued to the box where the Maharaja sat looking like a mouse caught between two cats. 'Rambha and Paras?'

Rati glanced at them and shrugged. 'I'm not worried about *that*. If it does become a problem, it won't, at any rate, be one for us. No, I mean Meenakshi. She's got a note.'

'I can't see any reason why she shouldn't receive a note,' said Shel. 'We must all guard against this tendency to unnecessary panic. It's getting out of hand.'

'Nothing to worry about, you think?'

'I think,' said Shel, 'that if we *do* need to worry, we'll find out soon enough. In the meantime, I suggest you enjoy the singing. Or,' he added with a wince, as one of the lords of Vraja hit a note calculated to make glass crack and birds fall from the sky, 'at least endure it.'

⚜

Nalini looked around the room. It wasn't large, but she could see that it had, in its original state, been impressive, if the impression its owner wanted to make was of someone who had visited an illicit Alchemical supplies shop and bought everything in sight.

'If this was where he received potential clients . . . ' Kamakshi ventured, but then compressed her lips and said no more. Kamakshi had never believed in the physical trappings of magic anyway, and years of chasing magical creatures around the Eastern Isles had only made her more inclined to use no tools other than a stick of chalk and a piece of string.

'*Look* at this place,' said Persis, indicating the overturned chair, the jar lying on its side with the colourful crystals inside spilling onto the ground, and the torn pages of a long-debunked spellbook scattering the room. 'There's been a fight.'

'The floor seems to have been scorched,' noted Nalini. 'Just like at Lord Das's house. That might be a sign that the Sprite was resisting.'

'The scorched floor might be a Sprite. What about the rest of this mess? There's been a physical fight.'

'Have you *seen* Sprites brawl?' asked Nalini. 'I have, and let me tell you, I can *more* than believe that a single Sprite made this mess while trying to resist his Summoner's orders.'

'He *was* being held here.'

'He isn't here now,' said Kamakshi. 'Any signs of where he might have gone? It'll be nice if we have confirmation before we invade Lord Das's estate looking for him.'

'We have to sort through this *mess*?' Persis asked dismally, looking at the scraps of paper swirling around in the light breeze the open door had admitted. Several of the scraps had writing on them. In keeping with the public perception of a magician, the writing was spidery and would probably need to be referred to an expert in graphology before any sense could be made of it.

'Certainly not,' said Nalini. 'What do you think junior magicians are for? We'll have some of them here to search the room.'

Meenakshi read the note again.

It was from the man known only as the Counsellor, who made it his business to know everything non-magical that happened in Madh, and nearly everything that happened in the rest of Pür. If Ravi had, instead of being Summoned, been bundled in a sack and spirited away on horseback, the Counsellor would have been able to name the culprit and identify the horse.

Meenakshi, one of the few people who was on good terms with him, had sent him an enquiry the previous day. She had left instructions for Gopali to send the reply to her as soon as it came.

> *Looked into the matter. Most of the people concerned*
> *have disappeared. One remaining. Junior porter;*
> *possibly overlooked.*

> *I've made the arrangements. I hope you know what you're*
> *doing. I've heard that Sprites are amassing in Rajgir. Do*
> *be careful.*

Chapter XII

'Authorizations from the Dangerous Beings Control Squad.'

'Thank you,' Nalini said, to the young woman who brought her the little bundle. 'Remember, don't discuss this with *anyone*.'

The woman, with a quick nod, left.

Nalini shut the door and turned around to find Kalban staring at her.

'What?' she asked.

'That's the woman who left the note for Rambha.'

Nalini stared at him. 'Don't be ridiculous. She's one of the Bureau's most capable junior officers.'

'I don't remember seeing her in Madh,' said Asmanajas.

'She works for our office in Rajgir . . . Kalban, are you *certain*?'

'I *saw* her. She is the one.'

'But she *couldn't* have mistaken Rambha for Vasundhara,' said Nalini. 'She's one of *us*.'

'We can worry about it later,' said Kamakshi. 'Nalini, unless you think she knows too much and we should call everything off until we've questioned her—'

'No,' Nalini said firmly. 'She's too junior to have had access to important information. I doubt she even knows what the authorizations are for. I just asked her to collect them and bring them here. We don't have time. We can question her later.' She unwrapped the bundle and sorted out the slips of paper. 'I've also got yours,' she said to Meenakshi and Kalban. 'I didn't tell them the details and I think they're assuming you're coming with us. Their fault for not asking for full information.' She shrugged. 'Authorization notwithstanding, *please* don't use deadly force against an immortal being if it isn't required. That'll be a lot of paperwork.'

'Don't worry,' said Meenakshi, folding her authorization up and tucking it into her satchel, which already contained a couple of useful books and some chalk.

Kalban carefully put his in his much larger bag, which was so full of magical supplies that it was bulging at the seams.

'I've *also* got permission from the Arcane Zoology Authorization Desk for you to take the griffon, as long as you ensure that he doesn't eat anyone.'

'He's a *herbivore*,' Meenakshi said. 'Why does nobody ever remember that?'

'We have backup teams from the Dangerous Beings Control Squad in the area,' Nalini went on. 'They won't get involved unless someone needs them. If anybody gets in trouble, send up a magical flare, and they'll come to you.' She paused and glanced at Meenakshi and Kalban. 'A magical flare will also draw the attention of the Inter-Realm sensors, as you know.'

'Kalban,' Asamanjas said, 'are you sure you want to do this? You *are* a Licensed Magician.'

Kalban shrugged. 'I won't touch the thing.'

'As long as you're certain. If you *do* get in serious trouble . . . we can handle the diplomatic disaster, if it comes to that. That's what Nalini's here for. Send up the flares if you need to. Don't get yourselves killed in an attempt to avoid the Inter-Realm sensors.'

'Give it twenty-four hours.' Kamakshi took over. 'If you've not found anything by tomorrow morning, don't waste any more time on it. We'll regroup and figure out what to do. Remember that we have a deadline . . . which might have been an unfortunate choice of words.' She glanced at the water clock on the windowsill. 'On that note, we'll open the portals in ten minutes. You're doing it from your room?' she asked Meenakshi, who nodded.

'All right,' said Nalini. 'Let's go. Good luck.'

Everyone dispersed. Kalban followed Meenakshi upstairs to her room.

Gopali and Saha were waiting with Chitralekha. All three of them looked, to varying degrees, disapproving. Kalban would have put the disapproval down to the day's expected doings, if it hadn't been for the fourth person in the room, standing as far as possible from the griffon.

'What's *he* doing here?' Kalban demanded.

'I told the guard not to let anyone in,' said Meenakshi. 'I have time for a quick word with him—'

'Wait,' Gopali said. 'I let him in. I told the guard I had your permission—yes, I know, I'm sorry, but it was either this or have him trying to climb in through a window and getting caught in one of the traps. I thought your mother might not like that,' she added to Kalban.

'I can speak for myself, you know,' Abhinav said.

'Whatever you want,' Meenakshi said, 'we don't have time now. Today's a free day. Go see the sights of Rajgir. There's a fine museum. Come back tomorrow.'

'I want to go with you. Wherever you're going now—I want in.'

'*Excuse* me?' said Kalban. 'Absolutely not. We're not taking you. You can't defend yourself against a Yakshini. Don't be an idiot. Stay *here*.'

'Kalban's right,' Gopali said. 'Look, Abhinav, other than your tendency to live in a madhouse where scorpions turn up under pillows, I have nothing against you. I don't particularly want to see you killed by whatever is waiting at the other end of the portal.'

'Mother would *never* agree,' said Kalban, with the air of one who had the deciding argument.

'That's why I didn't ask her,' said Abhinav, with the air of one who had a keen rebuttal.

'I'm *definitely* not taking responsibility for you, then. Go back. That's the end of the matter.'

'All set,' Persis said.

'Including your amulets,' said Kamakshi.

'I have confirmation from the teams in place,' Nalini announced. 'We're good to go.'

'I can't *believe* you took his side,' Kalban muttered to Chitralekha.

'I think it might be useful to have someone non-magical with us, that's all.'

'Only as bait.'

'Time!' Gopali called, putting an end to the argument. 'Clear the floor. Meenakshi, your coordinates.'

Everyone was out of the way and the order to clear the floor was only for form's sake, but Kalban took vindictive pleasure in seeing that Abhinav took a few steps back in any case.

Meenakshi glanced at the map and snapped her fingers. Light slashed the air, spun and widened into a portal.

'Go through,' Meenakshi said.

Kalban went first, Chitralekha and Abhinav on his heels. Meenakshi came last, with the griffon, and let the portal close behind her.

Kalban looked around. Meenakshi had brought them out at the edge of a cart-track. Ahead of them, it wound into an increasingly thick growth of trees; behind, the roofs of a village were just visible on the horizon against the pale blue early morning sky.

'What now?' Chitralekha asked.

'Now we wait,' said Meenakshi. 'Someone will be along to meet us. The Counsellor arranged it,' she explained, in response to Chitralekha's questioning look.

'You told him?'

'Who's likelier to know where Lord Das found his treasure? Don't worry, our guide won't be late.'

'There he is now,' Kalban said.

A lone man was making his way down the path. He was moving quickly, looking straight ahead, clutching his shawl closely around his shoulders—all marks of someone who had been told to have business with a sorceress and wanted to finish it as soon as possible and get back to his comfortable home.

'He looks like I feel,' Abhinav muttered.

'Nobody made you come,' Kalban snapped.

'That's not true. Rati made me come.'

'I *knew* it.'

'And *you* thought Rati was going to help us,' Meenakshi pointed out.

'Fan out,' Nalini said to the senior Dismisser from the Dangerous Beings Control Squad. 'Secure the perimeter. Block all portals. Make sure nothing and nobody physically leaves the estate until we're done.'

'That's a lot of perimeter to contain.'

'We'll be quick. Signal us when you're ready and we'll move in.'

Nalini went back to the front gate to join Kamakshi and Persis. Persis looked delighted to be there; it might have been a day at the fairground. Nalini could understand that. Stuck in a stuffy court like Melucha's, where they banned public magic at the slightest pretext and had absolutely no sense of humour when it came to the occasional spell gone wrong, although hemlock was regarded as a fine joke, it must be a relief to be among civilized people.

'The plan is simple. We'll go through the building first and look for the Sprite and any magicians. Don't worry about examining footprints and bits of paper. There's no need for us to waste time. The Maharaja's people will move in as soon as we're done and search for physical clues. And don't turn anyone into anything unnatural,' Nalini said. That seemed a sensible warning to issue, given who her companions were. 'Unless under extreme provocation, and I *do* mean extreme.'

'I doubt it'll come to that,' said Kamakshi. 'The family are all in Rajgir for the swayamvara. It's unlikely that the staff maintaining the estate are invested enough in Lord Das's plan to offer provocation to a magician.'

'Don't be too sure,' Persis said grimly.

Nalini led the way through the gates.

Since they had hardly tried to *hide*, most of the staff on the estate were gathered just inside the gates watching them. Once they entered, a tall man who must be the chief of them stepped away from the cluster and approached them.

He said, in a voice whose trembling belied his brave words, 'What is your business? My master does not allow any visitors in his absence.'

'I am Nalini,' Nalini said with exquisite courtesy, 'Head of the Inter-Realm Liaison Bureau. This is Princess Persis of Melucha, and Lady Kamakshi, one of the world's leading experts on magical animals. We have authorization from the Maharaja to search this estate.'

A man at the back of the gathering broke away and ran in the direction of the main house.

'Oh, dear,' said Kamakshi. 'How foolish.'

She gestured a portal into existence a few feet ahead of the man, who ran through it and found himself emerging from another portal a few feet behind. Before he could stop himself, he had run through the first again. He reemerged from the second, finally came to a halt and turned and trudged back to the gates, glaring at Kamakshi.

'I have a lot of patience,' Kamakshi said brightly, 'in case anybody else wants to try running away.'

Nobody else wanted to try running away.

'Please line up in an orderly fashion,' Nalini said briskly. 'These representatives of the Inter-Realm Liaison Bureau will take your names and ask you a few routine questions. Cooperation is not necessary, but it will be remembered in your favour if the matter comes up before the Inter-Realm Council.'

The forest met every qualification for being home to mysterious treasure and an angry spirit. As they went deeper into it, the foliage closed overhead, allowing only a faint greenish light to penetrate. There was no cheerful birdsong, no sound of crickets or frogs or lizards, no sound at all save a faint background hum that *might* have been insects, and the occasional distant roar of a predator.

'Can't one of you make some light?' Abhinav grumbled, when he tripped over a tree root. 'What's the *point* of being in the company of two magicians and a Celestial Dancer if I have to stumble around in the dark?'

'If there's a Yakshini here,' said Meenakshi, 'we don't want to draw her attention until it becomes necessary. No magic.'

'There *is* a Yakshini,' said their guide. He was ahead of Meenakshi, leading them in a single file through the undergrowth. 'Everyone knows that. *And* she knows we're here. She knows everything that happens in this forest. She's just waiting to see what we do.' He looked over his shoulder. 'A traveller from Khand went missing here. Three years ago. He *disappeared* into thin air. No trace was found of him except his shoes. The investigators *said* he was eaten by a tiger, but we all know who *really* took him.'

'There are *tigers*?' Abhinav asked, as one who was finding his immediate prospects bleaker by the moment. 'That roaring is *tigers*?'

'What did you *think* it was?' asked Kalban.

'I don't know! Sound effects!'

'Don't worry,' Meenakshi said dismissively. 'Mortal beasts like Celestial Dancers. They won't hurt us.'

'How did Lord Das get his treasure out past the Yakshini?' Kalban asked.

The guide scoffed. 'She doesn't care about silver and gold. There's something *else* hidden in her cave. We knew it was dangerous when we got near it. I'm no magician and *I* could feel it. Here's the river. We cross this bridge and we can get to the back entrance of the cave without meeting the Yakshini.'

River was a generous description for the trickle of water over moss-covered rocks. The bridge was a large, equally mossy log spanning the narrow expanse. The guide scuttled across without difficulty. He jumped off on the other side and beckoned to them to follow.

When Meenakshi stepped onto the bridge, there was a roar that *wasn't* a far-off tiger. The trickle became a sudden gushing torrent that covered the bridge. The griffon reared up, wings flaring in alarm.

Chitralekha hastily pulled Meenakshi back before she could lose her footing. The river dropped.

'That has never happened before,' said the guide, wide-eyed, from the other side.

'You didn't have magicians with you before,' Chitralekha said. 'If there is a Yakshini, and I'm starting to agree that there is, her sole purpose is to keep magicians from getting to the Fire of the East. We need to find another way around. Can you come back across?'

The guide put one terrified foot on the bridge. When the river stayed calm, he ran across and jumped down, panting.

'I don't know if there's another way to reach the back of the cave. The river goes underground further down. That route goes to the front of the cave.'

'And the Yakshini,' Kalban said. 'I suppose we don't have a choice but to face her.'

'I won't go with you all the way,' the guide warned. 'I'll take you to where the river goes underground. You need to find your own way after that.'

'Do I get a vote?' Abhinav asked.

'No,' Meenakshi snapped.

'Nobody made you come,' Kalban added. 'In fact, I distinctly remember telling you not to come.'

'I'm not a magician. I can cross the bridge with the guide, find this . . . Fire of the East, whatever it is—'

'And banish the Yakshini who's guarding it?' Chitralekha said. 'Don't be ridiculous.' She turned to the guide. 'All right, take us as far as you can.'

Windows and doorways blazed with light. The staff had been asked to vacate the premises, so as Nalini, Kamakshi and Persis went from one room to another, the only footsteps were their own, echoing through the high-ceilinged rooms.

So far they had found nothing. There were no magical residues and no signs of a Sprite or any other being from the Inter-Realm having been anywhere near the house or touched anything in it.

'Could we be wrong?' Persis asked, when they regrouped in the entrance hall after having examined the entire building including the stables and outhouses. 'Even if the Sprite's been taken away, if he had *ever* been here there would have been some signs.'

'I hope not,' said Kamakshi. 'We're running out of time to find Ravi.'

'Of course, we're not wrong,' Nalini said. 'Neither of you met the oily weasel Das. *I* did. He was hiding something.'

'First thrice-cursed and now an oily weasel,' murmured Persis. 'I wonder what you're going to call him next.'

'With you practically breaking down his front door looking for trouble, I'm not surprised Lord Das was hiding something,' said Kamakshi. 'We had better find it or there'll be no *end* of paperwork.'

'Maybe what he's hiding has to do with the treasure,' Persis said. 'Money is a strong motivator. Nobody knows exactly *where* the treasure was found. The estate is on the edge of public land. The Maharaja might ask for most of it to be put into the public coffers. And if it really *was* Amsuman's treasure, there are plenty of his descendants ready to claim a share, of whom Lord Das is *not* one.'

'That's *it*,' Kamakshi said. 'The treasure.'

'What?'

'Lord Das's treasure. If it *was* guarded by a Yakshini for hundreds of years, we would have found traces of her magic. So either we *are* completely wrong about it, or . . . '

'Or,' finished Persis, 'the treasure was kept somewhere we haven't yet looked.'

'You're the expert at secret rooms,' Nalini said.

'We should have brought Rati to make certain of finding one. I'll do my best. Kamakshi, you ought to have decent spatial sense after making your way through trackless wastes in search of firebirds. Is any of the rooms smaller than it ought to be?'

'This is as far as I go,' said the guide. 'You're on your own now. Keep going due north—you can't miss it when you get to it. Has anybody a compass?'

'I do,' said Abhinav.

Kalban and Meenakshi looked at him and at each other.

'What?' Abhinav asked. 'I thought it might be useful. I'm sure there's a spell that tells you which way is north.'

'You should go back with the guide,' Meenakshi said. 'He can take you to Lord Das's estate. Someone there will open a portal back to Rajgir for you. I don't think you should come with us. We don't know what we're going to find.'

'Or,' said Kalban, 'more importantly, *who.*'

'Go *back*? After I've come all this way? I'm not going anywhere.'

'Can't you make him go?' Meenakshi asked Kalban. 'You're older.'

'I'm older than you, and can I make *you* do anything?'

'Let him come,' Chitralekha said unexpectedly. 'We *don't* know what we'll find. He might be useful.'

Abhinav wasn't entirely certain he was pleased to have Chitralekha's vote.

CHAPTER XIII

'Definitely here,' Kamakshi said. 'We're losing at least four feet between this room and the next.'

'Then here it is.' Persis studied the wall.

Nalini and Kamakshi stepped back to give her room to work.

'I *can't* believe anyone would construct a secret room for Summoning here in Pür,' said Kamakshi. 'Magic isn't anathema here. Why not just Summon in the library like a normal person?'

'Lord Das's mansion in Rajgir is new,' said Nalini, 'but *this* building is old. I'm no expert, but it might predate the Inter-Realm Accord. If so, that would explain the *existence* of a secret Summoning room. As for why he used it . . . would *you* want it known that you were involved in the kidnapping and ransom of a Sprite? Persis, any luck? Don't worry if you can't find the way in. We'll take down the wall.'

'Let's try to avoid destroying private property,' Persis said cautiously, years in Melucha having made her more circumspect in the practice of magic than her friends, particularly when it came to giving cause for complaint. 'Give me a few minutes, I'm sure I'll find it.'

'We don't actually need to *blast* through the wall,' Kamakshi said, as Persis walked along it, tapping at intervals. 'Just a few bricks—and we can put them *back*. I can't answer for the tapestry—'

'*Look* at the tapestry,' Nalini said. 'We'd be doing Das a *favour* if we made holes in it. He ought to be grateful to us for giving him an excuse to throw it away. It was probably a wedding present from some great-uncle who must be humoured because he's terribly rich.'

'Not *helping*,' Persis said.

Nalini pulled up a chair and sat down to wait. Kamakshi, feeling far too restless to sit, went to the window.

The house hadn't been constructed with views in mind and there wasn't much of one beyond the hedge. A little scrubby grass quickly gave way to the forest.

Kamakshi knew all about forests. The Eastern Isles were about ninety-nine parts forest, the last part being given over to small cleared areas where the people lived in remarkably sophisticated settlements. Sophistication came in the good ways and the bad: the tiniest village Kamakshi had seen (Harkan, pop. 5) had an excellent plumbing system and the latest books and magazines delivered on request, but three-fifths of its population was constantly squabbling over the position of village chieftain while the remaining two-fifths wrote indignant essays about the state of modern politics.

Unlike her husband and daughter, Kamakshi had a fairly good grasp of people. You *needed* to have a good grasp of people to spend years exploring remote islands without getting yourself murdered by unfriendly locals.

People, whether the inhabitants of uncharted jungles or country noblemen from Pür, were the same everywhere.

'Why would Lord Das do this?' she asked slowly. 'It can't just be for the money—it's too great a risk for that.'

'Money is a strong motivator.'

'To help himself to treasure to which he might or might not be legally entitled, yes. Do you honestly see him risking the sort of trouble that would come from kidnapping a Sprite for the sake of a *little* more gold than he had already? And it might not even mean that, unless he's secretly magical—'

'Not a bit of it,' Nalini said.

'So he can't use the Fire of the East himself, and he can't sell it—not to any licensed magician or reputable gallery. He's not the sort of man to visit the forests north of Yauna to look for a tribe that isn't a signatory to the Inter-Realm Accord.'

'I agree with you about *that*. The man doesn't have the gumption.'

'Then if he did it, *why* did he do it?'

'Found it,' Persis said, before Nalini could answer.

Kamakshi turned to see. Nalini leapt to her feet.

Persis was pressing on a panel in the wall. It moved. There was an ear-splitting grinding noise. A section of wall slid back, revealing a dark space.

'*Oh*, they need to oil that,' Persis said. 'It's hardly secret with all that racket.'

Kamakshi could sense faint traces of Yaksha magic—explained by a pile of gold coins in one corner of the room—but those traces were almost overwhelmed by the more recent presence of a Sprite and the residues of Summoning magic.

She conjured a ball of light and shone it into the darkness. It revealed a Summoning circle on the floor.

'How did we not *sense* this?' Nalini said.

'There's a spell preventing magic from seeping out . . . this must be a *very* old room.' Kamakshi stepped inside and shone the light into all corners. 'There's been a Sprite here. *And* a magician.'

One side of the room had a desk and chair. There were a few scraps of paper on the desk. Persis went and flattened them out.

'It's some kind of modification to the Summoning spell. Doesn't seem to be stable.'

'Ravi escaped?'

'No, he would have turned up in the Inter-Realm and Rambha would have called off the search. I can't tell what this is meant for—there's not enough here. He must have taken the bulk of his notes with him.'

'And taken the Sprite as well.' Nalini sighed. 'He was here. We were right. They were here.'

'We didn't miss them by much,' said Kamakshi. 'The residues of magic are *strong* . . . it can't be more than a few hours since they left.'

'They must have known we were coming,' Persis said.

'How could they? Hardly anybody knew that. We didn't even tell Rambha we were coming here.'

Meenakshi, the griffon shuffling at her side, led the way through the trees. She had decided, after all, to borrow Abhinav's compass, much to Abhinav's smug satisfaction. Using magic would show her north, or up or any other direction she wanted, but it would also alert the Yakshini—if there *was* a Yakshini, she reminded herself firmly—and that was something she wanted to avoid as long as she could. Eventually, they would have to face her.

'Why are you all so scared of the Yakshini?' Abhinav whispered behind her. 'I thought Yakshas were a dime a dozen in Madh.'

'Neither of us Summoned her,' Kalban said, from where he was bringing up the rear. 'Her Summoner must be long dead. She's been trapped by their spell for centuries, which would be enough to make *anyone* cranky.'

'*If* there's a Yakshini,' Meenakshi said. 'Let's not get ahead of ourselves.'

'If there's a Yakshini. If there's the Fire of the East.'

'Isn't it past lunchtime?' Abhinav said. 'Did someone bring food?'

'I have oranges,' Meenakshi said. 'You can eat while you're walking.'

'Oranges? *Oranges?* Is that all the food you've got?'

'When about to encounter a potentially dangerous magical being,' Kalban said, with all the grimness Meenakshi had come to expect from him in such situations, 'it's best to eat lightly. Citrus fruits settle your stomach. *Everyone* knows that.'

'*Fine*,' Abhinav said. 'Give me an orange.'

Meenakshi stopped and fumbled in her bag. As she took out an orange, she heard something moving in the trees.

She put the orange in Abhinav's outstretched hand and turned in the direction of the noise.

The griffon cowered against her legs.

Since, unlike her more notorious predecessors in the art of Alchemy, she had been bound by the International Code of Sorcery, Meenakshi had been forced to replace several arcane ingredients of the spell with others obtained from a licensed Alchemical supplies shop. Madh had the best-stocked Alchemical shops in the Free Lands; all the same, the shopkeepers had too much regard for their own safety to deal in tiger's milk or cobra's venom.

The result of Meenakshi's efforts had been griffons that, while they looked impressively fierce and could screech eerily on request, had the appetites and general temperament of placid herbivores. This one was the mildest of them all, which was why Meenakshi had been allowed to keep it as a pet. The others were in Madh, deterring enterprising robbers who sought entry to the city's vaults.

'What?' Kalban hissed.

'Something's watching us. We must be close.'

Abhinav squeaked and almost dropped his orange.

'Is it the Yakshini?' Chitralekha whispered.

'We're about to find out.'

'That looks like the cave.'

Chitralekha pointed. It took a moment of peering through the trees before Meenakshi realized that what had seemed a shadow was really a narrow crevice in the rock.

'Slowly,' Kalban warned. 'There might be traps.'

They advanced cautiously, the dense undergrowth forcing them into a circuitous route. Meenakshi lost sight of the crevice as she ducked around a large and thorny bush. When she finally got around the bush, and the clump of fig trees after it, she found herself closer to the rocks than she had expected.

A carved statue loomed before her. It was a woman with a sword, twice as tall as Meenakshi. Its eyes seemed to burn with an inner fire, although the rest of the stone was encrusted with moss and lichen.

Something thrummed nearby. Meenakshi could feel the energy filling the air to overflowing.

'This is *it*,' she breathed. 'The Fire of the East. It's here. It *has* to be.'

She dimly registered Abhinav's look of alarm. Then Chitralekha caught at her arm. '*Meenakshi*. Remember, Class V Forbidden Magical Artefacts are forbidden for a *reason*.'

'I *know*,' Meenakshi said irritably. 'I'm not planning to *use* it.'

'When this is over, *give it to m*e. You promised.'

'I remember.' Meenakshi took a step forward. 'Let's go. Once we have the gem, I'll open a portal directly back to Rajgir.'

The griffon followed eagerly behind her as she went to the crevice. It liked treasure and dark places.

The opening was just wide enough for Meenakshi to squeeze through it into the tunnel beyond. The griffon bounded in after her. Chitralekha, made primarily of air and light, had no problem, but Abhinav looked like he was going to get stuck.

'Maybe the two of you had better wait outside,' Meenakshi said doubtfully, watching Abhinav struggle to get his shoulders through the opening.

'Don't even *think* it,' Kalban snapped.

He gave Abhinav a hard shove, sending him stumbling into the tunnel. Ignoring Abhinav's glare, he managed to get in himself by dint of turning sideways and wriggling.

Inside, the tunnel sloped steeply down. It quickly widened into a broad cavern. As they entered it, the light from the outside faded.

'We can't do this in the dark,' Chitralekha said.

'It doesn't matter any more. Whoever is guarding this cave knows we're here.'

Meenakshi raised her hands, and a ball of white light formed over each. Kalban did the same.

The cavern was large. The lights they had made illuminated distant walls, shining with dripping water. In the middle was an inscribed rock.

Meenakshi went to it.

'Here is the treasure of Amsuman,' she translated. 'Take freely of gold and silver, if you have found this place. Beware of touching the most precious jewel.'

Kalban bent to examine the damp sand of the floor.

'No footprints other than ours,' he said. 'I don't see how Lord Das's men could have come here.'

'Wait,' said Abhinav. 'I thought I saw another exit. Can you point the light over there?'

Kalban shone the light where he had indicated. A shadow showed a passage leading out of the cavern on the other side. The griffon was already there, scrabbling in the dirt. It put its head in the passage, and turned back to look at Meenakshi enquiringly.

'Griffons have an affinity for treasure,' Meenakshi said. 'Go on. Show us where it is.'

The griffon led them down a winding passage. There were tunnels leading to left and right, but Meenakshi didn't bother to count. It would distract her from paying attention to the hum in the air, that was growing stronger by the moment, and could either mean the Fire of the East or a powerful magical being—

The tunnel opened into another cavern, smaller than the first. The griffon bounded to a spot in the middle and turned to Meenakshi, lion's tail waving enthusiastically. Meenakshi hurried over and dropped to her knees.

'The *damp*,' Abhinav muttered.

Meenakshi ignored him. They must be under the riverbed by now; it was no surprise that the cavern was dank and musty.

There were definite traces of something heavy having been dragged from the place. The griffon, nosing in the dirt, came up with a gold coin in its beak.

'Good boy,' Meenakshi whispered. She turned to the others. 'There *was* treasure here. Lord Das must have taken it, like Nalini said.'

'Maybe he also took the gem?' Abhinav asked. He was shivering, and probably not from the cold.

Meenakshi doubted he could sense the magic now filling every bit of space around them. But there was an evolutionary instinct, a vestigial remnant of the days when humans had been living in caves such as this one and trembling at the thought of the jealous spirits who ruled the world, to recognize the presence of an unfriendly magical being.

The guardian of the treasure was waiting. Waiting to see if they would be content with the gold coin and leave, or—

She looked around. If it was true—if Nalini's suspicions were all true—

Then Lord Das must have known the location of the Fire of the East. He hadn't taken it—perhaps the guardian had prevented him—

It must be somewhere an unmagical person could recognize—

The griffon, having deposited the first coin in Meenakshi's lap, was rootling around for more. But it wasn't gold she needed.

She let the lights flare brighter. Something glinted at the back of the cave.

Meenakshi got to her feet.

As soon as she took the first step towards it, there was a rush of air and something else.

Kalban's lights went out. Meenakshi held onto hers only with a strong effort. The griffon screeched, deafening in the small space, and hid behind Meenakshi.

The figure of a woman was before her. She was taller than any mortal, filling the cave floor to ceiling. Her eyes glowed like lit coals. She held a sword that gleamed white in the darkness.

'Oh, look,' said the Yakshini, her voice the low rumbling of thunder. 'Here are some little magicians who walked right into my cave.'

CHAPTER XIV

'It's been many, many years since anybody tried to take the Fire of the East. You would have done better to stay away. It has a dark history. It was good for mortals when they forgot its existence.'

'Unfortunately, *everyone* didn't forget,' Meenakshi said. 'We need the gem.'

The Yakshini considered her for a moment. Then she said, 'Why?'

Meenakshi just managed to conceal her astonishment. In her experience, Yakshas didn't stop to ask existential questions, or indeed, any questions at all.

'*Well?*' said the Yakshini.

'It's complicated,' Chitralekha piped up from somewhere behind Meenakshi, and then fell silent when the Yakshini glared at her.

'A Celestial Dancer?' the Yakshini said. 'A Celestial Dancer helping two magicians and . . . ' The Yakshini paused and looked at Abhinav disdainfully. 'And that boy, whoever he is, invading my cave? A Celestial Dancer participating in a foolish attempt to claim the Fire of the East for a *mortal*? Have Rambha and Urvashi lost all control of their people in the centuries I've been trapped?'

'Someone's kidnapped a Sprite,' Meenakshi said.

'*Meenakshi*,' Kalban hissed. 'You don't just *tell* people *everything*.'

The Yakshini, however, relaxed. She lowered her sword, letting the tip rest on the cave floor. Steam rose where it touched the wet sand. After a moment, she leaned on the sword, driving the point further into the ground. There was a soft hiss.

'You must *hate* this place,' Chitralekha said. 'Damp— unpleasant—dark—smells like the underside of a rock. When did you last leave the forest?'

'I was Summoned here,' said the Yakshini. 'Here, in this cave. I *fought* my Summoner—oh, yes, I did. I would have killed her if I could have done. I would have ended her line . . . but she Summoned me with one of Nestor's Unbreakable spells.' She straightened. 'Do you think centuries of confinement have improved my temper? Do not try me, Dancer.' Then, turning back to Meenakshi, 'What's this about kidnapping a Sprite?'

'*Who* Summoned you here?' Chitralekha said, before Meenakshi could answer. 'You said *she*. I already knew it couldn't have been Amsuman. He had no magic at all.'

This time Chitralekha visibly quailed before the Yakshini's furious eyes.

'Try to distract me again and you'll regret it. I was one of the first Yakshinis given power by mortal fears. You, magician, answer me. Which Sprite has been kidnapped?'

'He's called Ravi. Vasundhara—the Princess of Pür—wants to marry him—'

'The men who came here for the gold were from Pür.'

'You *saw* them?'

'Of course I saw them. It was gold they wanted. I had no reason to stop them. They tried to take the stone, but they couldn't lift it from its place against my will. It would have done them no good. They had no magic to use it. They didn't know what it was until I told them.'

'You *told* them?' Meenakshi said. 'So this trouble is all because *you* were indiscreet?'

The Yakshini's eyes flashed. Her fingers tightened on the sword hilt.

'Can't you make her stop antagonizing the powerful supernatural being?' Abhinav whispered to Kalban.

'Nobody made you come,' Kalban snapped, not bothering to keep his voice low. 'You should have turned back with the guide. Meenakshi, all the same, he has a point. Try not to get us killed.'

'Tell me about the Sprite,' the Yakshini said.

'Vasundhara wants to marry him. Her grandfather—the Maharaja—said he would only allow it if Ravi attended her swayamvara and competed against everyone else. He was going to do it, but then someone kidnapped him. They're threatening to kill him if we don't give them the Fire of the East.'

'One less Sprite can only improve the world. Sprites are even more foolish than Dancers.'

'That's what Rambha says—not exactly in those *words*, but she says it was the Sprite's fault for falling in love with a mortal and he should have known better—'

'Rambha never was a fool.'

'But Rajgir—the city—it's *full* of Sprites. They've crossed over to the Mortal Realm in hordes. There must be a few hundred. A small army. They're *angry*. Nalini thinks they're going to revolt, *here* in the Mortal Realm, if Ravi is killed. There are people looking for him, but if they can't find him—'

'You want the Fire of the East to bargain for the Sprite's life.'

'Yes.'

'I will grant you that's a more interesting story than most have told who've come here. They've come wanting power, or wealth, or strength of arm—and yet that, despite your story, is what *this* comes to, isn't it? Power, or wealth, or strength of arm—or something similar, that you'll be giving the kidnapper, that you'll be keeping for Rambha, if I let you take the Fire of the East.'

'We won't actually give the kidnapper the gem—Nalini says it's just leverage—'

'I don't know who Nalini is. I have orders,' the Yakshini said. 'My Summoner is gone. Her grandchildren's grandchildren must be gone. But her orders stand. Nobody takes the Fire of the East. You're a powerful magician. I'll grant you that. That you can even keep your magic working . . . ' She indicated Meenakshi's lights with the hand that wasn't holding a sword. 'Working, however feebly, against my will, in *my* place, shows it. But you must be *very* young. *I* am very experienced. You can't win. The Dancer won't stand against me. That boy over there *can't* use magic against my will. As for the other boy, I don't know why you even brought him . . . '

She trailed off, studying Abhinav. Then she turned her baleful gaze on Kalban.

'Yes,' she said softly. 'Oh, yes, I see.' She turned back to Meenakshi. 'There you have it. You cannot win this fight. Those two boys I will make an example of, but I'll let you go if you don't fight me. What will it be?'

Abhinav opened his mouth, and closed it again hastily when Kalban kicked him in the shin.

'Be *quiet* and let Meenakshi handle it,' he said. 'There's no other option now.'

Meenakshi showed no sign of fear. 'What will you guard if there's nothing here?' she asked.

'It doesn't matter. I'm bound to this cave.' Again her eyes flickered to Kalban and Abhinav.

Meenakshi followed her glance, looked at her, *felt* the background hum of power from the Fire of the East—

And a piece of the puzzle fell into place.

'*Really?*' she asked the Yakshini. 'How can you tell? It was over five hundred years ago and was an *entirely* different person.'

'Five hundred and fifty years,' said the Yakshini. 'And I can tell. I've thought of her. I've thought of her every *day*.'

'*What* can you tell?' Kalban asked.

'You,' the Yakshini said, raising her sword with purpose. 'And that boy with no magic. You are of *her* line.'

'The magician who Summoned this Yakshini and trapped her here must have been one of your ancestors,' Meenakshi explained rapidly. 'You do have some cause for complaint,' she went on, addressing the Yakshini, forestalling any remarks from Kalban. 'But is your vengeance worth your freedom? Do you want to be trapped here forever?'

'My Summoner is dead. I *am* trapped here forever.'

'I can free you.'

In the silence, Kalban could hear the air sizzle faintly at the edge of the Yakshini's sword.

Then she said coldly, 'You're lying to save your friends. Do you take me for a fool? This is one of Nestor's Unbreakable Summoning spells.'

'*You're* out of date. It's been at least two hundred years since Nestor's Unbreakables were all broken. It takes a powerful magician.' Meenakshi shrugged. 'Kalban could do it if you weren't blocking all magic in this antisocial way. I can do it. Now. A magician trapped you here. I'll set you free.'

'Do you think *that* will even the score? Do you think it will make up for five hundred and fifty years in this silent dripping darkness?'

'I don't care about the score. I'm asking what you want to do *tomorrow*. Still be trapped here?'

'I can't let you take the Fire of the East. I won't be responsible for putting it in the hands of a magician.'

'What's your freedom worth?' asked Kalban. 'Do you want to spend the rest of eternity guarding this damp cave? Or would you rather wait until the next magician comes? Someone who wants to *use* the Fire of the East for world domination?'

The Yakshini glanced at him and back at Meenakshi. 'How do I know you're telling the truth about what you want?'

'I'm asking *nicely*. I *could* simply undo the spell and then Summon you back—with a spell that nobody *can* break, at least not with today's state of magic.'

'You could *try*.' The Yakshini's sword blazed with white fire. 'I am Mahendri, the most terrible of my kind.' Chitralekha gasped. 'You've heard of me, haven't you? My anger is the wrath of heaven. All creation trembles before my name. I will not give you the Fire of the East, mortal. The risk to the world is too great.' The griffon chose that moment to poke a tentative beak out from behind Meenakshi. Mahendri stared at it. 'What manner of beast is that?'

'A . . . a griffon,' Meenakshi said.

'A griffon . . . a legendary guardian of the world's greatest treasures. An imaginary creature brought to life. Was it your alchemy that gave it breath?'

'I suppose you could put it like that.'

'It doesn't seem to care about the Fire of the East.' The griffon had another gold coin in its beak, which it dropped at Meenakshi's feet. 'If you wanted to create something to help you find treasure, you failed. Gold is the least of the world's precious things.'

'Perhaps it is, but even gold is more precious than powerful magical artefacts. You know that's true. Try to use them, and it ends on a battlefield. Who would want that?'

'Those who trapped me here would have wanted it. *You* want the stone. Don't deny it.'

'I want it,' Meenakshi agreed. 'I'm curious about it. But I don't think it's treasure. Five hundred and fifty years is a great deal of time for mortals. Most of us have learnt not to milk tigers. Those who haven't are reduced to kidnapping Sprites to achieve their ends.'

Mahendri looked like she was wavering.

Meenakshi pressed her advantage. 'Lord Das knows the Fire of the East is here. You told him what it is yourself. You told everyone with him. It won't stay a secret much longer. You might defeat me, but there'll be others. At some point, you *will* lose. Let me have it now. I'll make you the same promise I made Chitralekha—once this is over, I will give it to Chitralekha. It'll be safe in the Inter-Realm, out of mortal hands, forever.'

'Forever doesn't last. Better to destroy it.'

'I couldn't,' Meenakshi admitted.

'You're truthful, I'll give you that.'

'Once you're free, *you* can make certain it's safe. From the Inter-Realm, where you belong.'

'So be it,' Mahendri said with a sigh. 'I have dwelt here for many years. Release me, give me your word that you will see the Fire of the East safely out of the Mortal Realm, and I will let you take it.'

'Will you let us *all* go unharmed?'

'I will.'

Meenakshi opened one of her spellbooks and found the incantation. Sparks glowed and fizzled in the damp air.

The hum of magic grew stronger. Light filled the cave.

Mahendri, for the first time in centuries, was free. She stood taller, towering over them, her sword a line of blinding light.

'Promise me,' she said to Meenakshi. '*Promise* me that when you have retrieved the Sprite, you will take the stone back from his kidnapper and give it to the Dancer.' Then, with a slight smile, she added, 'Or destroy it yourself. I'll give you that much leeway.'

'I hope it doesn't come to the kidnapper having the gem,' Kalban said. '*That* would be a disaster.'

'*Promise me,*' the Yakshini insisted, ignoring Kalban. 'You must not let the Fire of the East remain in the Mortal Realm.'

Meenakshi nodded. 'I promise.'

'I am Mahendri. If you break your promise, my vengeance will be terrible.'

'I don't intend to break it.'

'Very well. I will stand aside, but I'm not the only thing protecting the stone. There's magic. I don't know what it is. Good luck.'

Mahendri wasn't there.

⚕

This time Nalini didn't go to see Lord Das alone.

That had been attempted. He had lied, *far* more boldly than she had expected for such a craven. It was time for stronger measures.

She had him invited to the High Commission of Madh. Politely as it was worded, an invitation from the Head of the Inter-Realm Liaison Bureau was simply a warning that the Dangerous Beings Control Squad would shortly be sending Dismissers to escort one to the meeting and it would be far wiser to already be at the meeting when they arrived.

A substantial reception committee was waiting for Lord Das when he came. In addition to Kamakshi and Persis (who, as Princess of Melucha, had no business being there, but who was going to question a sorceress known for turning people into pigs?) she had invited Asamanjas, the Maharaja, Bahuka, the Minister for Inter-Realm Affairs, and Tejas, the Minister for Law and Order.

She hoped Lord Das would feel awkward and intimidated as soon as he entered the room.

If he did, he hid it well. He glanced around, cocked an eyebrow at Asamanjas, inclined his head politely to the Maharaja, and sat in the chair Nalini indicated.

'This is something of an inquisition,' he said. 'Isn't it excessive?'

Nalini glanced at Persis, who was standing by the door. Lord Das hadn't noticed her; he started when she spoke.

'Lord Das, as I am certain your staff have informed you by now, this morning we visited your country estate, with the authorization of the Maharaja, to search for clues to the missing Sprite.'

'Oh?' said Lord Das, calm air vanishing. It was hard to quaver on a monosyllable, but somehow he managed it.

'Would it surprise you, Lord Das,' said Kamakshi, from the other side of the room, 'to learn that Princess Persis found a hidden chamber in your country house?'

Lord Das turned awkwardly in his chair to face Kamakshi.

'Did she? It's an old house. It's been in my family for three generations. Before that it belonged to a distant—and inferior, *highly* inferior—cadet branch of the Maharaja's family. I'm afraid I don't know nearly all its secrets.'

'Someone must have known about the hidden chamber,' said Persis. 'We saw signs of its having been occupied until quite recently.'

'Ah.' Lord Das looked at Persis and then looked around wildly—at the Maharaja and the ministers sitting on either side of him, at Asamanjas, at Nalini, and then back at Persis. 'I have, as you know, been in Rajgir for the swayamvara. I left the estate in the charge of one of my most trusted employees—I will speak to him about this—'

'Lord Das,' Kamakshi said, 'the chamber was used by a magician.'

'A Summoner,' Persis specified. 'A Summoner who Summoned a Sprite. Unfortunately, none of us had the skill to ascertain *which* Sprite it was—'

'*Ah,*' said Lord Das, considerably more cheerfully.

Nalini just managed not to grind her teeth.

'*However,*' Kamakshi went on, 'as you are no doubt aware, by fortuitous chance, the Master Sorcerer and the Master of the Royal Academy are both in Rajgir at this time. We can also have the Chair of Summoning and the Chief Dismisser of the Dangerous Beings Control Squad brought in from Madh.'

Fortunately, Lord Das didn't say, 'Oh.' Nalini might have screamed.

'Lord Das, let me explain,' said Asmanjas, taking charge at a signal from Nalini. Asamanjas might have as little magical ability as Lord Das, but he had ample experience of the combination of coaxing and menace required to administer Madh. 'You will, of course, be within your rights to put us to the great inconvenience of calling several people, including the Master Sorcerer, from their legitimate business to find out whether the Sprite Ravi was Summoned to your country estate. But if you do that . . . there will be questions asked. By, among others, the Chief Celestial Dancer, who, as you are no doubt aware, is in the city at this moment.'

Lord Das looked chastened, as anyone would when confronted by the threat of the Celestial Dancer who had broken the power of some of the most infamous dark sorcerers in the history of the Mortal Realm.

'Rambha doesn't *really* care about you,' Nalini said. 'You're not a magician. The only use you might have had for the Fire of the East was to sell it or give it to someone else.'

'I'm sure you weren't stupid enough to go to all this trouble without having a buyer lined up,' said Asamanjas. 'Give us a name.'

Lord Das, looking from one person to another, wilted under Nalini's gaze. He shook his head wildly. 'I can't—I *can't*.'

'Nonsense,' said Nalini. 'You can do anything if you put your mind to it. Would you rather write them down? That's even better. I'll fetch you some paper.'

'No—you don't understand. I'll give you the name of the person who did the Summoning—'

'We know that he was a Summoning Service freelancer. Where is he now?'

'I don't *know*.'

'He left,' Persis snapped, at the end of her patience. 'His name is Rishi—we know that—we know you got him through the Summoning Service, and we know he kept the Sprite in the hidden chamber on your country estate. What we don't know— what you *are* going to tell us, if you don't want to spend the rest of the day as a pig—'

'You can't do that!' Lord Das protested.

'Can't I? Try me.' He quailed before her gaze. 'Tell us whom you intended to give, or sell, the stone to, and tell us where the Sprite is.'

'I *can't*. I don't know where the Sprite is. I told Rishi you were coming,' Lord Das said hastily. 'I told him—I sent a message, there's a great deal I have to deal with—the running of a country estate, I'm sure you understand—so I use the postal portals regularly. Rishi sent me word that he had an alternate location and he would take the Sprite and leave. He didn't tell me where.'

'What about the Fire of the East? Who wants it?'

'It's a magician. I don't know who it is, I swear. I'll tell you everything if you grant me immunity.'

'We just told you,' Nalini said impatiently. 'Rambha doesn't care about—'

'Not Rambha.' Lord Das was looking at the Maharaja.

'Oh,' said the Maharaja.

Then he said nothing. The silence stretched.

Asamanjas cleared his throat pointedly.

'Oh, very *well*,' said the Maharaja. 'Whatever you've done, Das, we'll overlook it—just this once—*if* you tell us all you know.'

A slow smile spread across Lord Das's face, matching the gleam in his eyes. 'Since I have your word,' he said. 'There were rumours of a treasure in the jungle—deep in the forest, so it would be considered public land, but nobody else was looking for it, or likely to. I went. There was gold. Jewels, pearls, plate . . . all sorts of things. I helped myself.'

'I *knew* it,' the Maharaja muttered. 'You didn't even pay the full tax on it, I'll bet.'

Asamanjas cleared his throat again.

'Administrative details. Not important now,' said the Maharaja. 'Go on.'

'There was a gemstone, shining, even in that dark cave, as though it held a galaxy of stars. I would have taken it—I knew it must be valuable—but a Yakshini appeared and told me I couldn't have it. She said it was the Fire of the East—some ancient gem, too powerful for mortals. I had enough gold—I didn't want the gem, not if it was going to bring magical disaster with it. I left it and came away. I swore all the people who'd gone with me to silence, but *somebody* must have talked. A few weeks ago, I received a letter telling me that the Sprite—Ravi—needed a place to stay.'

'And you jumped at the chance?'

'I didn't *want* to. I have nothing against magicians, but I know the danger of magic. But the letter said he would come to my house, and if I let him stay with me then he'd be grateful to me when he became Princess Vasundhara's consort. If I didn't . . . the letter-writer knew I hadn't had a right to take the gold—Amsuman's treasure—and he would tell the Maharaja.'

'Ah. The letter-writer had you coming *and* going. So you let the Sprite stay with you.'

'Then there was another letter,' went on Lord Das, who, having begun speaking, apparently had no intention of leaving off. 'It told me to engage Rishi to Summon the Sprite. I promise, I just thought the letter-writer was interested in the swayamvara and wanted the Sprite kept out of the way to give his candidate a better chance. I had no idea they were after the Fire of the East.'

'I think he's telling the truth,' Asamanjas said reluctantly.

'I *am*. I *swear* I am.'

'So the Fire of the East *is* where you thought,' the Maharaja said to Nalini. 'But the Yakshini is real too. She might prevent Meenakshi and Kalban from getting it.'

He didn't sound as though he believed it himself. Nalini shook her head at once.

'There's been no signal flare, so they're not in trouble. Kalban would have sent one up even if Meenakshi didn't. That being the case . . . it's likely that they'll be here, soon, with the Fire of the East. We need a better plan.'

CHAPTER XV

Meenakshi hesitated.

The Yakshini was gone, but magic still thrummed through the cavern. She could feel it. She could sense the Fire of the East, but also something *else*—whatever was protecting it.

She took a few steps forward. In a small carved niche in the wall rested the gem. It was larger than she had expected—she had been picturing something the approximate size of a pigeon's egg, but the piece of fire agate was as large as her hand. The surface was smooth—polished by some long-past magician, or perhaps by sand and water over the years—and it gleamed as though lit from within.

'Something's going to happen if I take it,' she whispered.

Chitralekha said suddenly, 'Wait. Abhinav—you take it.'

Meenakshi looked at her in astonishment, Kalban in outrage, and Abhinav said, 'What? No! I want nothing to do with it.'

'Meenakshi's right. There must be a trap—Mahendri told us as much—and if so, she and Kalban may need to use magic to get us out of trouble as soon as the gem's been removed from its place. If you think I'm allowing a sorceress on the watchlist to use the Fire of the East—'

'Your watchlist is pointless bureaucracy,' Meenakshi said. 'I've not done anything to deserve to be spied on. I'm not going to use the gem.'

'You are *not* holding that thing while using magic, especially when we might be in danger. That might be too great a temptation.'

'Chitralekha's right,' Kalban said reluctantly. 'Let Abhinav take it. He's safer than any of us—he can't do anything with it. Maybe he won't even trigger the traps.'

Meenakshi looked unconvinced, but she shrugged and stepped away.

'Go on, Abhinav,' said Chitralekha. 'Take it.' She looked from Meenakshi to Kalban. 'And you two be prepared for whatever might happen.'

'Are you certain this is a good idea?' Abhinav said. 'What if it destroys anyone non-magical who touches it by turning them to a pile of smouldering ash?'

'That's unlikely. It's a minor risk, and one I'm *far* more willing to take than chance a powerful magician being tempted by its magical potential,' Chitralekha said.

'Thank you.'

'Don't *worry*,' Meenakshi said. 'Amsuman must have handled it, and it didn't turn *him* into a pile of smouldering ash. Just take the thing and we can leave.'

Abhinav reached out and picked the stone up with both hands.

He made a face. 'It's heavier than it looks.'

Then the floor gave way beneath them and they were plunged into darkness.

✝

The Master of the Royal Academy faced the Head of the Inter-Realm Liaison Bureau across the table.

To say he was angry would be an understatement.

He had been angry when, as students at the Academy, Paras had beaten him by two and a half marks in their Licence Tests. He had been angry when a member of his staff had made him look bad by conspiring in a half-baked fashion with a gang of witless students. He had been *angry* when he had been called, against his will, to Rajgir to attend a pointless royal event. What did he care if Princess Vasundhara was having a swayamvara? *He* didn't want to marry her.

Now, he was *furious*.

'You did this *without* telling me?'

Nalini shrugged. 'It was difficult to tell you. You weren't here. And, quite frankly, I have no obligation to tell you what I do in my work.'

'I can understand that you didn't inform me of Kalban's presence—'

'I should *hope* so,' said Nalini, who, as the Master of the Academy knew, excelled at drawing people off on tangents. 'He's a fully licensed sorcerer *and* a member of a foreign court. It's really none of our business what he does.'

'Oh, if I could believe *that*,' snapped the Master of the Academy. 'But Meenakshi is neither licensed nor a foreigner. She is still, nominally at least, under my supervision. You had no right to ask her to locate a Class V Forbidden Magical Artefact without my consent.'

'Wouldn't you have consented if we had asked? Given the seriousness of the situation, which I don't think I need to state to you, since you must have seen for yourself how many Sprites are in Rajgir and how eager they are for trouble? Would you really have objected to the Master Sorcerer's daughter fulfilling her responsibility to Pür by doing what she could to prevent an Inter-Realm war?'

'You're exaggerating,' snapped the Master of the Academy.

'Am I? How many Sprites did you count outside this building on your way in? Besides, you must see that *someone* was bound to find the Fire of the East soon. That pestilential Das knows its location, several members of his staff were *with* him on that wretched expedition, and at least *one* of them has been indiscreet about it. It was only a matter of time before more magicians went looking for one of the greatest treasures of history. Better that it's found first by those we can trust.'

'You trust Meenakshi and Kalban, do you?'

'Don't you?'

'Yes,' he said reluctantly. 'I do. As much as I trust anyone. But with the *Fire of the East*? If it's everything it's rumoured to be—'

'It is, according to Rambha.'

'That might be too great a temptation for anybody.'

'That's not important now,' Nalini said.

'*Excuse* me?'

'At any rate, there's nothing we can do about it. We need your help finding Rishi.'

'Rishi?' said the Master of the Royal Academy. '*Who* is Rishi?'

'He studied at the Academy. Finished his Fellowship, specializing in Summoning, six years ago, and he's been working as a freelance magician ever since. Lord Das engaged him through the Summoning Service to kidnap the Sprite. He's gone to ground somewhere—Lord Das *doesn't* know where, or so he claims. We're keeping a watch on him but all the same it's quite likely that Rishi will be able to communicate with him without our knowing. He's got no family that we've been able to locate, no close friends in Rajgir.'

'So you want to speak to his Fellowship supervisor?' the Master of the Academy guessed.

'Yes, exactly. I don't need to speak to him *personally*. I just need to know where Rishi is likely to have gone with a Sprite he was holding against his will.'

'All right. I don't know offhand, but I'll have someone find out.' He paused. 'What about the Counsellor?'

Nalini grimaced. 'I'd rather not. I doubt it would do any good. He doesn't usually bother to keep track of magicians—especially those outside Madh.'

Abhinav, clutching the Fire of the East to his chest, stumbled upright. He was standing on rocks, slippery-smooth. Water sloshed around his shins. His trousers clung unpleasantly to his legs.

He was in total darkness. But at least he wasn't alone. From sundry sounds, he could make out that Kalban, Meenakshi,

Chitralekha and the griffon were getting to their feet. He *hoped* it was only Kalban, Meenakshi, Chitralekha and the griffon.

'Where are we?' he said aloud.

Light flared to the right and left of him. It looked like Kalban could use magic again.

'A tunnel . . . under the cave,' said Meenakshi.

'A tunnel containing something terrifying that will eat us?' Abhinav asked. 'Because that's usually the kind of tunnel that's found under a booby-trapped Yakshini-guarded cave in books.'

The griffon screeched.

'Shhh,' Meenakshi said, patting it absently. 'Let's keep the silly suggestions to a minimum.' She raised her hand, lighting the tunnel walls. 'There's an inscription over there. A symbol of some sort.'

'Amsuman's seal,' said Chitralekha, who was nearest.

Kalban turned sharply. 'Then this must be the tunnel we read about—the tunnel leading from the statue of the Goddess of Speech in the Kos Desert.'

'The tunnel that takes three days to walk through?' Meenakshi asked. 'It's not much of a trap, is it?'

'It would be if you weren't a magician,' said Kalban.

'We're here without any food or water,' Abhinav said. 'As would be the case for anyone who came through the tunnel and consumed all their food and water on the way, expecting to be able to walk through the forest to civilization at the other end. I am *definitely* not drinking whatever this is at the bottom of the tunnel, so I'd call it an excellent trap. We're all going to starve here.'

'No, we're not,' Kalban said impatiently, gesturing at the air in front of him.

A slash of light appeared, shimmered and disappeared.

Kalban tried again. The same thing happened.

'What is it?' Meenakshi said.

'I can't open a portal to Rajgir. You try.'

Meenakshi waved a hand. A slash of light appeared, grew into a circle, lasted just long enough for Abhinav to get his hopes up—

It fizzled out.

'This place is cut off,' Meenakshi said. 'Magically. We can use magic inside it, but we can't reach *out*. Chitralekha, can you—'

'I can't get out,' Chitralekha said. 'I tried.'

'Then we have to *walk* out?' Abhinav said in disbelief. 'For three days, with only some oranges? I refuse to do it. I'd rather just give up and stay here. Somebody's bound to come looking for us.'

'See if there's a way to go back up,' said Meenakshi. 'If people were meant to come through this tunnel and find the cave, there must be something.'

Kalban cast light on the ceiling.

'There,' Abhinav said, pointing. 'There's a trapdoor. But it's ten feet up. There must be a ladder somewhere.'

'There is.' Chitralekha was examining something near the tunnel wall. 'Or, at least, there *was*. Somebody must have cast a preservation spell on it for it to have lasted this long in running water . . . but, all the same, I don't think it'll take any of you.'

Abhinav waded across to her. The ladder, if it could still be called that, had rotted over the centuries. Only a few rungs remained, and they didn't look like they would bear his weight.

'It won't hold me.'

Meenakshi shrugged. 'That's a minor issue.'

Abhinav felt the ground moving away under his feet and a rush of air. He yelped, and then realized he was hovering just under the trapdoor.

He turned to glare at Meenakshi. 'A little *warning* next time?'

'See if you can open the door.'

Abhinav grasped the iron ring and pulled. Then he pushed. The wood of the door looked as aged as the ladder, so it ought to have given way under his efforts, but it stayed solidly in place.

'Get him out of the way,' Kalban said.

Abhinav was splashed back into the water. Before he could express his opinion of magicians, *these* magicians, and magic in general, a flash of white light filled the tunnel.

When it faded, the trapdoor was still closed.

'That must be the trap,' Kalban said. 'When the Fire of the East is removed from its place, the trapdoor is sealed. The entire tunnel is sealed, physically *and* magically.'

'So we wait?' Abhinav asked.

'Of course not,' Meenakshi said. 'Time's running out for the Sprite. There must be a way to get to the end of the tunnel quickly.'

'Can you open a portal to the end of the tunnel? You said you could use magic inside the tunnel.'

'Not without knowing where it is. I might open the portal into solid rock.'

'And cause a major landslide in the process,' Kalban explained. 'Which is why we can't risk doing it.'

'All *right*,' Abhinav muttered. 'I'm not an *idiot*. What are we going to do, then?'

Kalban and Meenakshi both glanced at the Fire of the East.

'*No*,' Chitralekha said. 'Absolutely *not*.'

'I could break the spell and have us back in Rajgir in a *minute*,' Meenakshi said.

'And you could get Ravi back and send all the Sprites *in* Rajgir forcibly back to the Inter-Realm, possibly even Rambha herself, and are you certain you would stop there? It's not worth the risk.'

Meenakshi sighed. 'All right. Alternatives.' She looked around, and then splashed through the water to the far wall of the tunnel to run her hands along it. 'There are cracks,' she said. 'Small ones. That must be where the water comes from. We're under the river.'

She turned to Kalban.

Kalban shrugged. 'How, though?'

'There's the ladder . . . or what's left of it.'

'Are you certain you can control it?'

'Do you have a better idea?'

'No. Fine. Let's go.'

'What?' Abhinav said. 'Wait—no—what's happening? What are you planning?'

'We're getting out of here,' Meenakshi said. 'Kalban, you're the expert. You deal with the ladder.'

'*One* time,' Kalban said. '*One* time I used the water gate to the Academy, and that's going to follow me for the rest of my life, isn't it? You're never going to let me forget it.'

'*And* you commandeered a sloop as a *child*. Just make us something that'll last long enough to get to the end of the tunnel.'

'What's going *on*?' Abhinav demanded, as Kalban sloshed past him to the ladder, which he pulled down and dumped in the water. 'Excuse me? Is someone going to explain?'

'A lesson I've learnt over many centuries,' Chitralekha said cheerfully, 'is that when magicians aren't explaining, you usually don't want to know. Meenakshi, do you need help?' Meenakshi was examining the walls of the tunnel closely, pressing her fingers into the cracks.

Meenakshi mumbled something about the thickness of the stone and how far the spell extended.

'I have a notebook,' Abhinav offered, 'if you need one.'

'Is there anything you *didn't* bring?'

'Food,' Abhinav said.

'You'd think that would be the *first* thing to put in if you're packing for a forest adventure.'

'I didn't know we were going to end up in a dripping tunnel.'

'Out of my way!' Kalban snapped.

Chitralekha hastily backed away to the tunnel wall. Abhinav pressed himself against the wall on the other side. Meenakshi, on the other hand, splashed into the middle of the tunnel.

'What sort are you making?' she asked. 'Flat bottom?'

'That'll be easiest, given the supplies. Get the griffon out of the way.'

Meenakshi clapped her hands. The griffon bounded to her and then shook itself, spraying water on everyone.

'Now I'm *wet*,' Abhinav complained.

'Don't worry,' said Kalban. 'You'll get wetter soon.' He looked back at Meenakshi, who nodded, and then down at the remnants of the ladder. 'How many places am I going to escape like this?'

Kalban opened his hands, which filled with light, and directed it at the ladder. There was a creaking and groaning and splintering of wood.

A raft, large enough to hold all four of them and the griffon, lay where the ladder had been. It looked extremely rickety. Abhinav had doubts of its ability to get them even four feet, leave alone down the entire length of the tunnel.

'I did my best,' Kalban snapped, in response to Abhinav's look. 'I didn't exactly have a lot to work with.'

'I didn't say anything.'

'It'll do,' Meenakshi said. 'Get on.'

Abhinav noticed suddenly that the level of water in the tunnel was rising. It had been lapping around his shins; now it was to his knees.

'I don't like this.'

'Get on the raft.'

Abhinav scrambled on and went right to the middle. Chitralekha and the griffon followed. Kalban, after checking the underside of the raft one last time, climbed on.

'All right, we're ready.'

Meenakshi took another look at the roof of the tunnel.

'It *should* hold.'

Then she waded through the water which was now well above her knees and clambered onto the raft. It dipped and swayed.

'Are we too heavy?' Abhinav asked warily.

'We should be all right. Nobody move too much.'

'Do we need to paddle?' Abhinav asked, as the water rose another four inches. The raft sat low in the water, but it *was* floating. 'I don't think we'll save a lot of time that way.'

'No, but that reminds me . . . ' Meenakshi reached into her satchel and pulled out one of the orange sticks. As she held it, it grew until it was four feet long and an inch and a half thick. 'Here.' She thrust it at Abhinav. 'Try to keep us from bumping into the walls. And hold *on* to the Fire of the East. This is all for nothing if we lose it. Kalban, are you ready?'

'Go,' Kalban said.

The water rose in a surge. An irresistible current tugged at the raft, whirling them away down the tunnel faster than Abhinav would have thought possible.

CHAPTER XVI

'My lady, a note from the Prince. He requests an immediate response.'

Persis took the envelope with a nod of thanks. She tore it open, ignoring the messenger's wince—he must be horrified at her failure to check the seal for poisoned needles, even on a letter from her husband—and pulled out the single sheet of paper inside.

'Oh,' she said, looking over it. 'Oh . . . oh *my.*'

Kamakshi, across the room, raised her head. 'What? Is something wrong?'

'No, I . . . ' Persis looked at the messenger. 'Tell the Prince everything's fine.'

'That's all, my lady? He thought there might be a written response. He told me to wait for one.'

'Everything's *fine.* Thank you. Goodbye.'

The messenger, acutely aware of Persis's reputation *and* the fact that he was standing on the sovereign territory of Madh, which had an infamously lax attitude to the regulation of magic, bowed and left the room. Persis looked around to make certain they were alone.

'Abhinav's gone with them.'

'Abhinav? Your son, Abhinav? Gone with whom?'

'Meenakshi and Kalban. Shel hadn't seen him all day, but he says he didn't think anything of it—he assumed Abhinav must be out enjoying the sights of the city. But when he didn't show up at dinner time, Shel instituted inquiries, and Rati—do you remember Rati? I think you've met her.'

'She came here to speak to Nalini. I saw her then. She seemed vaguely familiar . . . is she the one who doesn't like you?'

'Most of them don't like me.'

'Is she the one who supported a rival claimant to the throne?'

'Most of them supported a—oh, never mind. You'll know her if you speak to her. Rati confessed that she'd urged Abhinav to insist on accompanying Meenakshi and Kalban.'

'But how did she know?'

'It appears she got a lot of information out of Kalban. I'm sorry,' Persis added, as Kamakshi groaned. 'Something *happens* to him in Melucha. He's awkward and uncomfortable and he has the backbone of a jellyfish. It's like he's just *waiting* for someone to pop out of a trap and stab him.'

'We can talk to Kalban about discretion when they're back. Why on *earth* would Rati think it was a good idea to send Abhinav with them? She didn't *seem* like a raving lunatic.'

'Rati . . . people in Melucha in general . . . they don't understand how things work in Madh. Or Pür. They think, since magic is so widely accepted, being a magician must give one special status.'

'The Maharaja's not a magician.'

'He's the Maharaja. And Paras *is* a magician. You must admit Madh looks that way to outsiders. The Governor of the Southern Provinces is nearly always the Master Sorcerer, and the person with the next highest status is the Master of the Royal Academy—'

'The Master of the Academy needn't be a magician.'

'In theory, I suppose, a professor of Mathematics or Philosophy or History could rise to the position, but how often does it *happen*? Oh, I *know*. I've spent years in Madh, remember. I know you can get on perfectly well if you're not a magician—most of the priests aren't—and I know exactly why it's so important that the Governor should be a powerful magician and it's got nothing to do with controlling those who aren't magical. But Rati has never been to Madh. She supports Abhinav over Kalban for the throne . . . '

'And she thought Abhinav could . . . improve his status . . . by going with Meenakshi and Kalban to get the Fire of the East.'

'That's my guess.'

Kamakshi shrugged. 'He'll be fine. He's not alone.'

'Yes, I only hope he has the sense to—oh, what is it *now*?'

Someone was knocking urgently.

Persis waved at the door, which burst open. 'What?' she snapped.

'Lady Kamakshi. Princess Persis.' This time it was one of the staff from Madh, unperturbed by her irritation. 'The Maharaja requests you to attend him at the palace immediately.'

⚜

An eddy caused the raft to bang hard on the tunnel wall. It shuddered.

'You're not doing your *job*,' Kalban barked at Abhinav.

'I'm sorry,' Abhinav snapped back. 'I was completely unprepared for the speed, we seem to be caught in a miniature riptide, and I've never been in this tunnel before in my life. Would you like to take over?'

'It must be almost over,' Chitralekha said. 'We must have come at least twenty leagues by now. A person couldn't walk much more than that in three days in this tunnel in the dark.'

Meenakshi, still sitting at the stern controlling the current that propelled them forward, said, 'Yes, it feels like we're—'

'Slow down!' yelled Abhinav. 'Slow down, I see a—'

The raft hit something and *finally* broke, dumping them all into the water. Luckily, it wasn't over anyone's head, though they were dragged along several feet before Meenakshi managed to stop the undertow. They came up spluttering.

'Where are we?' Meenakshi asked.

There was a screech from the griffon. It had managed to make its way to a ledge.

Kalban cast a light on it.

'Stairs,' he said. 'This must be the end.'

'*Finally*,' Abhinav said, still coughing. 'I was about to be sick. I just hope nothing's blocking the door at this end.' He scrambled onto the ledge, shivering in his sodden clothes. 'There *is* a door. No sign of how to open it. There's just a stone with a crystal in it. Please don't let there be some riddle we have to solve. I'll be *very* angry.'

Kalban climbed up next to him. 'Didn't Amsuman's will say something about entering the tunnel?'

'It said you need a magician's aid.' Meenakshi was casting some spell that was making the water recede. 'I have to undo it,' she said, in response to Abhinav's look. 'If the Tatini goes off course it might ruin the year's crop before someone manages to fix it. My uncle will *never* let me hear the end of it.'

'I can't find a way to open the door with magic,' said Kalban.

Meenakshi, with Chitralekha's help, scrambled onto the ledge. 'Just blast it—no, wait.'

'What?' Kalban asked.

'It's been hundreds of years. The entrance might be buried in sand.'

'So we're *stuck* here?' Abhinav asked.

'We're not stuck. We'll have to be careful. There'll be a way . . . there always is.'

Meenakshi climbed up the stairs and studied the crystal. She poked it, pulled it, and shot a jet of light into it. It didn't react to either of the first two. The jet of light vanished into the depths of the crystal.

'*Oh*,' Meenakshi said.

'Is that a *good* oh?' Abhinav asked Kalban.

'I think so.'

'It's a magical artefact,' Chitralekha said warily. 'Meenakshi, *don't* use it if you don't know what it does.'

Abhinav thought she would have done better to make that warning *before* they let one of the most unpredictable young magicians of the Free Lands examine the thing.

'It's not dangerous. It's just a conduit to the outside.'

'You can blow the sand away from the entrance?' Abhinav asked.

'I can do better.'

Persis and Kamakshi were the last to arrive.

Paras and the Master of the Academy were glaring at each other. Nalini was deep in conversation with the Minister for Inter-Realm Affairs, while the Minister for Law and Order appeared to be making some sort of impassioned plea to the Maharaja. Vasundhara was standing apart from everyone else, holding a folded sheet of paper.

Rambha was nowhere to be seen.

'Good, you're here,' the Maharaja said brusquely. 'Minister, *thank* you for your views, but you know as well as I do that we can't *ban* Sprites from Rajgir . . . No, I can't *help* what trouble they're making. Complain to Bahuka, it's his responsibility to see that they don't. Vasundhara, perhaps now you'll tell us what's happening?'

'I had a letter,' Vasundhara said. 'It was left outside my door— nobody saw who left it.' She unfolded the paper and read.

I know that you're going to have the Fire of the East by tomorrow morning. Don't think you can fool me. I'll know if it's a fake. I won't be giving you time to invent some other way to deceive me. Tomorrow, at noon, the Fire of the East will be left in the garden of Tara the Starchaser's Memorial. Then the Memorial will be emptied of all people, magical, non-magical and immortal alike. Do this or you won't see the Sprite again. Once I have the Fire of the East, I will release the Sprite.

'We can't do it!' the Maharaja said. 'We can't *give* him the Fire of the East. We'll be in violation of every section of the Inter-Realm Accord.'

'That's not important yet,' said the Maharani. 'We'll come to it. First, what *is* important is that nobody outside this room had any idea that we asked Meenakshi to find the Fire of the East, or that Kalban was helping her. *Somebody* has been indiscreet.'

'Oh, dear,' murmured Persis.

The Maharani raised her eyebrows. 'I refuse to believe it's you, so either you told someone deliberately, or . . . '

'No, I didn't tell anyone. But one of the members of Shel's court badgered it out of Kalban—I just found out myself!' she said, when the Maharani looked horrified. 'However, I know Rati, and she has her faults but I don't think she would ever conspire to put the Fire of the East in the hands of a rogue magician.'

'But she might have *talked*,' said the Maharani. She turned to the two ministers, both of whom were writing furiously. 'One of you go and see Rati and find out if she told anyone. Wait. Given the . . . unique views . . . people have in Melucha, it's best not to send a magician. Tejas, you're not magical, are you?'

'Not a bit. I studied Political Science at the Royal Academy.'

'Excellent. You go to the Meluchan Embassy, talk to Rati, *politely*, see what she can tell you. We need names. Report back here when you're done. Paras, we need to secure the Memorial in a way that the kidnapper won't notice when he comes to collect the ransom.'

'Wait—what about Ravi?' Vasundhara said.

'We'll *get* him. That's why we're going to all this trouble. But we are *not* going to put such a powerful magical artefact in the hands of a criminal. We'll arrest the kidnapper and make them tell us where they have the Sprite.'

'What if they won't tell us?'

'That's why we have Rambha. Paras, what do you need?'

'Shut down the Memorial now,' Paras said. 'It's a popular place for moonlight walks, isn't it? Have everyone cleared out and put guards around it. Kamakshi, Persis—are you busy? No? Good, I'll need your help. Nalini and the Minister for Inter-Realm Affairs, keep Rambha occupied.'

'I have a *name*,' muttered the Minister for Inter-Realm Affairs.

'I took the trouble to memorize the first man's name, but since the Maharaja changes the responsibilities of his ministers almost every year, I realized it was an exercise in futility. *You*,' he added to the Master of the Academy, whom he had never addressed by any other title in over twenty years, unless it was *back-alley faker*. 'I assume you have your people finding the Summoner? I can't believe it's taking you so long. Clearly the Academy has fallen from the high standards of efficiency it used to maintain.'

'Oh, go lay your traps in Tara the Starchaser's Memorial,' snapped the Master of the Academy. 'You worry about your business and leave me to handle mine.'

'It *would* help if we could locate Rishi,' said Nalini.

'I don't know what to tell you. His parents are from Khand—the Chair of Summoning went there *personally* to speak to them and his sister. He's been corresponding with them as usual. I have the letters now.'

'What can I do?' Vasundhara asked.

'You,' the Maharani said firmly, 'have to prepare for the next part of the swayamvara.'

'Oh, come *on*.'

'The swayamvara doesn't stop. *You'll* be otherwise occupied at noon tomorrow.'

⚔

Abhinav had no idea what Meenakshi was doing. Kalban obviously did, but all requests for information had been met with the curt response that he shouldn't have come, he needn't have come, and *having* come he shouldn't expect Kalban to stop to answer questions.

Chitralekha, naturally, was unconcerned. Why should *she* worry? Even if they couldn't get out, she only had to wait five years or five hundred years or however long it took for someone to find the tunnel.

It was growing uncomfortably warm in the underground space. At first, Abhinav had been glad of whatever in Meenakshi's magic had raised the temperature, since he had been thoroughly wet and cold. But now, his clothes were still damp, perspiration was breaking out on his brow, and there was nowhere for him to sit except on the edge of the platform with his feet dangling in the receding water.

The Fire of the East was in his satchel, carefully wrapped in the spare shirt he had brought, though Meenakshi and Chitralekha had both assured him it wasn't going to break. He was taking no chances.

It was odd carrying a magical artefact. It ought, from everything he had been taught about magic, to feel uncomfortable, even dangerous, but although Meenakshi, Kalban and Chitralekha had been casting occasional sidelong glances at his satchel, Abhinav himself felt no different than he would if he had been asked to carry any other large, heavy and inexpertly polished fire agate: mildly irritated.

'All right, it's done,' Meenakshi said, none too soon in Abhinav's opinion. 'We can go now.'

'What *took* so long?' Kalban said.

'I had to be *careful* with the construction, unless you wanted to be trapped in here forever. Just shove the door. It's been weakened enough, it'll open.'

Kalban did.

The bolt splintered and the door sprang open. Abhinav screwed up his eyes, prepared to be assaulted by the brightness of the sun in the desert after hours trudging through a gloomy forest, walking through a gloomy cave and almost being turned into goo against the walls of a gloomy tunnel. But the light that came through the opening was faint and silvery.

'It's *late*,' Abhinav said in astonishment.

'Were you expecting to be home in time for dinner?' Kalban asked coldly. 'We had twenty-four hours . . . We'll be back before dawn.'

Kalban stuck his head out of the opening. Then he ducked back inside to tell Meenakshi, 'This may end up being even more of a tourist attraction than the griffons. And a safer one.'

'If people *will* insist on trying to pet them . . .'

'You said they're herbivores,' said Abhinav, edging away from the griffon on the ledge.

'So they are. Even rabbits will bite if you keep poking them to make them spread their wings.'

'Rabbits don't have wings . . . unless rabbits are very different in Madh.'

'You know what I mean.' Meenakshi clicked her tongue at the griffon. It clattered across the rock to her and followed Kalban out the door.

Abhinav picked up his satchel.

As soon as he looked out, he knew what Kalban had meant about the tourist attraction—and he also knew why it had grown so warm in the tunnel. He was amazed that they hadn't all been baked to a crisp. Meenakshi had melted the sand covering the door into a staircase leading up, with glass walls that prevented the rest of the sand from falling into the gap.

It wasn't, however, the kind of nice, shimmering almost-crystal that it would have been in a story. The glass was uneven, with jagged edges and wicked-looking points. Abhinav was devoutly thankful that he had had the sense to wear stout shoes.

'I don't want to know what the griffons are like, if this is *safer*,' he said, going up.

At the top, he clambered out onto a large sand dune—and found himself staring into a pair of gigantic eyes that glittered in the moonlight. He yelped in surprise.

'The statue of the Goddess of Speech,' Kalban said. 'We should send a team to dig it up, when we get back. It looks like it's still intact.'

'The Chair of History and Archaeology will love you forever.' Meenakshi, the last to come up, looked at the statue and then up at the sky. A large shadow passed across the stars. Abhinav was terrified for a moment before he realized it was the griffon wheeling. 'There's something happening here.'

Kalban and Chitralekha both turned to Meenakshi sharply.

'Happening?' Kalban demanded. 'What do you mean?'

'I don't know. I can sense something.'

'Is it just the Fire of the East?' asked Chitralekha.

'No, I could sense *that* down in the tunnel. There's something else—'

'Not now,' Kalban said firmly. 'No investigations and no time wasting. Whatever is here has probably been here since Amsuman buried his treasure hundreds of years ago. It can wait a few days. Let's get back to Rajgir. Open a portal.'

CHAPTER XVII

Meenakshi was first through the portal. As soon as she stepped into her study, Gopali, who had been waiting in the bedroom, pounced on her.

'At last!' The griffon brushed past her to find its bed. 'Vasundhara was about to send out a search party!'

'We're well in time.'

'Yes, and I can see you've had some adventures. At least you're not dripping on the carpet. We *would* hear about that.' Gopali looked Meenakshi up and down. 'There have been developments. You need to go to the palace. Vasundhara said at once, but you can take the time to change into something dry that doesn't smell like the rainforest. *And* you,' she added to Kalban. 'Don't bother to go to the Meluchan Embassy, just borrow something from the Master Sorcerer's room—'

'He's half a foot taller than me,' Kalban protested.

'And you call yourself a sorcerer! *Find* something and make it fit.'

She turned to Abhinav.

'I have extra clothes,' Abhinav said hastily, holding up his satchel. 'But they're wet, too. And . . . '

'Oh. *Oh.*' Gopali turned to Chitralekha, who was last through the portal. 'You gave it to *him* to hold?'

'We can honestly say that no magician has laid hands on the Fire of the East,' Chitralekha said calmly. 'When Rambha learns about this and threatens to end the world, that's something in our favour.'

'Can Rambha end the world?' Abhinav asked warily.

'No, she can't,' Gopali said. 'And *you* . . . ' She looked at Chitralekha. 'I understand the reasoning. Let's hope Rambha does, if it comes to that. We have to move quickly. Abhinav, you should go home—wait, no, not home, the Minister for Law and Order is going to want to speak to you. He's downstairs. And he can take custody of the stone if we're aiming to keep magicians from touching it. *Then* we can send Abhinav home.'

'Your mother is furious with you, by the way,' Saha added cheerfully. 'With both of you. Kalban for talking to Rati—'

'She didn't give me a choice!'

'A sorcerer *makes* a choice,' Saha said. 'And with Abhinav for potentially endangering the whole plan by insisting on going along to do something for which he was utterly unqualified. Her words, not mine.'

'Oh,' Abhinav said dismally.

'And if you think *that's* bad, wait until you hear the contents of your father's note. And *you*,' she added to Kalban, 'until you speak to the Master Sorcerer. Now *go*—Kalban, go and get some respectable clothes on. Abhinav, go downstairs. Chitralekha, go back to the Inter-Realm or wait here, I don't care. Meenakshi, hurry up and find something to wear. Something *comfortable*,' Saha said with emphasis.

'Is there any possibility of something to eat first?' Kalban said hopefully.

'I'm sure we can get you something at the palace. *Go.*'

Gopali waited only until Abhinav and Kalban had left the room before rounding on Meenakshi. 'Chitralekha's telling the truth? You didn't touch it?'

'I didn't.'

'Did you use it?'

'No. I'm not stupid.'

'Did you *want* to use it?'

Meenakshi made a gesture of exasperation. 'The cavern was booby-trapped, and we were stuck in a magically sealed tunnel with no apparent means of escape. Of *course*, I wanted to use it. But I *didn't*. We would have been here hours ago if I had, believe me, and this entire problem would have gone away by now.'

'To be replaced by a far bigger problem,' Gopali murmured. She looked at Chitralekha. 'Was she all right?'

'She was in control of herself. So was Kalban. As far as *that's* concerned . . . I wouldn't say there's no need to worry. But aren't there bigger problems?'

'There are indeed,' Gopali said. 'Meenakshi, hurry up and get dressed. You're needed at the palace.'

⚔

Dawn, and the next event of the swayamvara, was an hour away. Vasundhara was dressed for it. She wasn't, as even Meenakshi could tell, happy about that. Meenakshi didn't blame her. She would have been grumpy too if she had been woken while the stars were still out to have her hair braided with alternating strings of jasmine and pearls.

Abhinav wasn't there. He had protested being sent back to the Meluchan Embassy at first. Then Gopali had pointed out that he could by that means postpone seeing his mother until she had had time to get over some of her anger at his rank idiocy.

After witnessing Persis's reaction to Kalban, Meenakshi was fairly certain she understood why Abhinav had decided that discretion was the better part of valour. Persis hadn't been able to really let herself go, since the clock was ticking—and, given the Maharaja's fondness for toys, the water-clock was dripping. But she had made full use of the little time available to her. Kalban was now occupied in trying to evade her notice.

Paras had spread an architect's blueprint of Tara the Starchaser's Memorial on the table. He, Kamakshi and Persis were bent over it, whispering and rearranging a handful of chess pawns.

'He said not a single magician or Ravi dies,' Vasundhara reminded everyone unnecessarily. She had been doing so at intervals since Meenakshi's arrival.

'We don't know that it's a man,' Meenakshi said.

'If it comes to that,' said one of the ministers, 'we don't know that it's a *mortal*.'

He was holding the Fire of the East, so it must be the Minister for Law and Order. Paras, Nalini and the Maharaja had agreed that it was best, since they had managed it so far, to continue to allow no magician to lay hands on a Class V Forbidden Magical Artefact.

'That isn't important,' said Paras. 'Between us, we can take care of everything. I've got a plan.'

He clapped his hands. An image of the blueprint projected itself on the ceiling.

'All right,' said Paras, causing labelled, glowing dots to appear on the map. '*Here* is where we put the Fire of the East. We'll have a non-magician do it—'

'I'll do it,' Vasundhara offered.

'You, my dear,' said the Maharani, 'will be observing the results of the athletic and equestrian competitions. Between all the events, qualifiers and finals, that won't be done before the middle of the afternoon.'

Vasundhara groaned. 'Can't I put a decoy in my place?'

'If representatives from every country in the Free Lands could come here to attend your swayamvara, the least you can do is to be physically present.'

'I'll do it,' said the Minister for Law and Order.

'No, you have another task,' Paras said. 'I want you with the Captain of the Guard. That's going to be our visible perimeter. Look, here.' A faint yellow ring appeared around the outside of the Memorial, at what would on the ground be about fifty yards away.

'The kidnapper isn't going to believe for a moment that we don't have anyone watching,' said Persis. 'So we'll *give* them someone watching. As many guards as you like, Minister, with swords, shields, battleaxes, those sticks with spikes on them . . . any weapons, so long as they make a good show.'

'We can't start a battle in the middle of the city during the Princess's swayamvara!'

'Nobody expects you to. That's just the distraction. Our expectation, since the kidnapper must be a magician—or, at least, have *employed* magicians—is that he, or she, will open a portal into the Memorial and bypass the guards.'

'But we're going to be careful nonetheless,' said Kamakshi. 'The Chief Dismisser, the Master of the Royal Academy, Kalban and I will be standing among the guards, in disguise, ready to act if there should be a suitable opportunity.'

'The rest of us,' said Paras, 'will take up suitable hidden vantage points inside the Memorial grounds. We've marked out spots from where we'll be able to observe the Fire of the East without being seen ourselves, unless the kidnapper should open the portal right next to one of us.'

'If that happens,' Persis said, 'we're in luck. Whoever it is, incapacitate the kidnapper, send up a flare, and everyone else will be there to help. Here are the locations—Meenakshi, up here behind this statue—Nalini, on the other side, concealed by the tree—Minister for Inter-Realm Affairs, you'll be under the western arch—'

'What?' said the Minister for Inter-Realm Affairs. 'No! I'm having nothing to do with it. And neither should the Head of the Inter-Realm Liaison Bureau. If Rambha finds out—'

'If all of us do our jobs correctly,' said Persis, 'Rambha won't have to find out anything. The Master Sorcerer, meanwhile, will be here, directly behind the statue of Tara the Starchaser. The kidnapper, if they've got any sense, won't risk using magic to pick up the stone without examining it first. If they don't spot any of us, they'll walk into the Memorial and come to the centre, at which point everyone—'

'Except me,' said the Minister for Inter-Realm Affairs.

'Good grief, man,' said Nalini impatiently. 'Do you think Rambha will be any angrier about *you* being involved in this than the Master Sorcerer? She probably won't even *notice* you.'

'I *beg* your pardon.'

'Oh *dear*,' said the Minister for Law and Order, looking around for a suitable corner to cower in.

'Tejas,' said the Maharaja, 'while they're sorting this out, let's discuss the disposition of the City Guard.'

'Your Majesty, I *demand* that you forbid them from involving me,' said the Minister for Inter-Realm Affairs. 'And, for that matter, Nalini—'

'The *disposition* of the *City Guard*.'

'Or, better yet, anybody at all. This is a stupid plan.'

'Now, see here—' said Paras angrily.

'Let's take a walk,' Asmanjas said to Meenakshi. 'This is going to be a massive argument. We might as well order some early breakfast while they settle it.'

'Do you think it'll take that long?'

'Probably longer. There goes the Master of the Academy about the ice staircase incident. It's been twenty-five years and he *never* fails to bring it up. This won't end quickly.'

True to Asmanjas's prediction, those who wanted early breakfast had finished it, and the first light of the new day was filtering through the curtains, before the argument was over.

'Now,' Paras said calmly, as though he hadn't ten minutes previously called the Master of the Royal Academy a fraud, a charlatan, and a two-bit country juggler, 'as we discussed, the Minister for Inter-Realm Affairs will be concealed by the western arch. The Minister for Law and Order and the Captain of the City Guard will nominate a non-magical member of the Guard to take the Fire of the East to the central plinth of the Memorial and leave it there.'

'Once the kidnapper reaches the central plinth,' Kamakshi said, 'and if nobody else has had cause to do so before then, Nalini will send up a flare. That will be the signal for all magicians to move in. It'll take all of us to prevent whoever it is from escaping with the Fire of the East. This is the time,' she added, 'if we want to call in anyone else.'

'From Madh?' asked the Master of the Academy. 'The Chairs of Alchemy and Summoning?'

'Maybe, but I was thinking more of magicians from other countries who are in Rajgir already for the swayamvara. There are some members of the Yaunic delegation—'

'No,' said the Maharaja. 'This is complicated enough. I'm not involving more people. Tejas, bring the stone. We'll put it in the vault until it's needed.'

'Everyone—except Vasundhara and the Maharaja—meet here one hour before noon,' Paras said. 'Now get back to wherever you're supposed to be. There's no need to make Rambha—or the kidnapper—suspicious.'

Kalban was having a hard time buckling on his breastplate.

He wasn't accustomed to using a breastplate. As a child, he had been trained in swordplay and archery, and sundry other martial arts, as befitted the heir to the throne of Melucha. Subsequently, as befitted a sorcerer, he had come to look on armour as an unnecessary encumbrance to the freedom of movement that was an advantage in a magical duel.

Unfortunately, disguising himself as a member of Rajgir's City Guard required armour.

The Captain of the Guard had never liked Kalban, regarding him as a potential Meluchan spy even when he had first visited Rajgir as a ten-year-old in Paras's household. Kalban wouldn't go so far as to say that it was a direct consequence that he had sent Kalban a uniform and armour that was three sizes too big, but . . .

Actually, Kalban *would* say that, and *did*, accompanied by an unflattering description of the Captain of the Guard that included some new words he had learnt from the Master of the Academy that morning.

'What do you think would happen,' said a voice from the door, 'if the Privy Council heard language so unbefitting the Prince-Heir?'

Kalban scowled at his brother. 'What do you want? If you have any questions, go and ask Mother. If you think I'm telling anyone *anything* after what she had to say on the subject this morning—'

'I *did* have questions, but now I'm just feeling sorry for you. Do they not make guard uniforms in your size? You look like a child dressing up . . . Which, I suppose, you *are*.'

'Go away, Abhinav.'

'Can't you magic it to your size?'

'That would require that I know more about the design and construction of armour than I actually do. Go *away*.'

'You know, you should be grateful to me,' Abhinav said, coming into the room. 'If I *hadn't* been with you, either you or Meenakshi would have had to touch the Fire of the East.'

'Oh, come *on*,' Kalban snapped. 'You've been listening to too many stupid stories from Rati and people like her. Do you honestly think that the reason we didn't want a magician to touch a Class V Forbidden Magical Artefact is that as soon as you do you become evil and want to take over the world?'

'No, actually, I just thought that being evil and wanting to take over the world was a magician's default state. Tell me, then, why is it so important for a magician not to touch a Class V Forbidden Magical Artefact?'

'Because of the Inter-Realm Accord.' Kalban finally succeeded in buckling the breastplate, though he doubted his ability to move in it. 'A magician has to *touch* a magical artefact in order to use it. They won't work without physical contact. The fact that no magician touched the Fire of the East, or even tried to, is proof for Rambha that we only retrieved it due to exigent circumstances, not to make use of it ourselves. Of course, if we'd touched it, we could have made the argument that we touched it without using it.'

'*Can* you touch it and not use it?'

Kalban threw his hands up in despair or tried to. 'It's a fire agate, not a mind control stone! Either Meenakshi or I could have taken it off you in the tunnel if we'd really wanted to. Now go *away*. I have to figure out how to put on my boots.'

'You should have done that before the breastplate. How are you getting to the palace?'

'Opening a portal from my bedroom, and no, I *don't* care what the Privy Council would think. I'm not appearing in public looking like this. And before you ask, I'm not taking you with me. If you want to come, ask Mother.'

'I'll just walk to the palace,' Abhinav said with dignity. 'I'm sure I'll get there before you figure out how to do up your boots.'

Kalban scowled at his brother's retreating back before turning his attention to his boots.

In the end, he managed to get them on. He picked up the helmet—no sense wearing *that* until it was absolutely necessary—and opened a portal.

Since nearly everyone was watching the races, the palace was empty. Kalban got to the antechamber where everyone else was gathered without being noticed. Abhinav was standing outside the door, looking grumpy.

'Mother told me to go and watch the races,' he said.

Walking past his brother into the antechamber was one of the most delightful sensations Kalban had experienced in some time.

He wasn't the last. Meenakshi, out of breath and just barely tidy—and with far less excuse, since she was wearing normal clothes—was a few minutes after him.

'Sorry,' she gasped. 'Chitralekha just *wouldn't* stop telling me about how important it is that we don't let the kidnapper get away with the Fire of the East.'

'Yes, we all know that,' the Maharani said. 'We'll have one final run-through of the plan and then everyone can get in place.'

'Don't we need to get the gem first?' said Meenakshi.

'I have it,' said the Minister for Law and Order, hefting the bag he had put the stone in after taking it from Abhinav.

'No, you don't.'

'I assure you, I took it out of the vault myself.'

'I don't know what you took from the vault,' said Meenakshi, 'but that isn't the Fire of the East. I just spent the better part of a day being near it. I know what it feels like. That's not it.'

There was a moment's dead silence.

Then Paras snatched the bag from the Minister for Law and Order and upended it on the table. A large fire agate fell out. He and Persis bent over it.

Kalban hadn't examined the original in detail, but as far as he could tell, it *looked* the same—

But—

He wouldn't have noticed it if Meenakshi hadn't said it, but—

'She's right,' Persis said a moment later. 'This one's a fake.'

CHAPTER XVIII

'Oh, this is bad,' moaned the Minister for Inter-Realm Affairs. 'This is so bad. This is *worse* than anything I thought might happen. We don't even know *who* has the Fire of the East now—'

'Can *somebody* stop that man *whining*?' Paras snapped. 'Preferably before I turn him into a frog? We *can* find it. We need to look at it logically. Who had access to the vault?'

'It needs two keys to open,' said the Maharani. 'There are two copies of the first key. I have one and the Maharaja has the other. There's only one copy of the second key and it's held by the Minister for Finance. The vault is sealed to magic—no portals in or out. And there are guards. Eight guards along the passage leading to the vault, four outside the vault itself.'

'Plenty of failsafes,' said Paras. 'And the thief couldn't have known in advance that we would put the Fire of the East in the vault. So the logical conclusion is that someone took the *real* Fire of the East and substituted the fake before it was put in the vault.

Persis and I examined the stone when the Minister for Law and Order brought it. It was the real one then.'

'But there was nobody else in the room after that,' protested the Minister for Law and Order. 'The same people who are here now.'

'And the Maharaja and Princess Vasundhara,' Paras said. 'Yes, I'm aware. That means one of *us* knows something about it.' He looked at the Maharani. 'Could Vasundhara have taken it? She's in love with the Sprite. She might resort to extreme measures to get him back.'

'I don't know,' the Maharani said reluctantly.

'I knew all along this was a bad idea,' moaned the Minister for Inter-Realm Affairs. 'Some of the most powerful magicians alive today are in this room and one of them has the Fire of the East. Rambha is going to *incinerate* the Inter-Realm Accord. This is bad. This is *so* bad.'

'Wait,' Nalini said, when Paras turned and glared at the minister. 'Ignore him, Paras. Remember he lives in Rajgir. We have to make allowances. Persis, is your son still waiting outside? The other one,' she added, when Persis looked at Kalban.

'I suppose so. Why?'

'Do you think he talked?'

'We can have him in and ask. I doubt it, though. But there's a more pressing question. What are we going to do about the ransom demand? The kidnapper will be expecting *something*.'

'Can we give him the fake?' Asamanjas asked.

'Any magician who examined it would know it was a fake. We don't have time to turn it into a Class V Forbidden Magical Artefact.'

'But we have time to turn it into a Class I Magical Artefact,' said Meenakshi. 'It'll fool the kidnapper from a distance. Not forbidden, no trouble with Rambha or the Dancers.'

'That means we can halve the number of magicians at the Memorial,' said Kamakshi, 'while the rest of us track down the real gem. Abhinav,' because by then Persis had called him in, 'does anyone—anyone at *all*—know where you went or what you did?'

Abhinav looked around at everyone. 'What happened?'

'Answer the question,' Persis said.

'I don't think so—well, other than Rati, and my father seems to have guessed a *lot* without being told, from the lecture he gave me this morning. I didn't tell anybody else—I've not even had *time*,' he added indignantly.

'Good enough for now,' the Maharani said. 'We'll figure out who's responsible later. Who's going to the Memorial?'

'The Ministers and the Master of the Academy,' said Paras. 'And they can turn the stone into a Class I Artefact first. Even that charlatan ought to be able to do a good enough job to fool the kidnapper long enough for him to approach the stone and be identified. Everyone else, stay here. We can't risk the Fire of the East being in the hands of a rogue magician. If we can't trace it in an hour, we're going to have to sweep the city.'

'Rambha will know if we sweep the city,' said the Minister for Inter-Realm Affairs.

'That can't be helped. We have to find the Fire of the East no matter what.'

Kalban caught at Meenakshi's arm. 'You made a promise to the Yakshini,' he said in an undertone.

'I know,' she replied calmly. 'Don't worry. We'll find it. Whoever's taken the Fire of the East hasn't done it with the intention of hiding it in a cave for five hundred years. Abhinav, if you're not doing anything else, find someone to open a portal to the Madh High Commission and bring Chitralekha here. She might have some ideas.'

꣓

The shadows had shrunk to almost nothing. Noon, or near it.

Vasundhara knew she appeared tense, no matter how much she smiled and waved at the crowd. Fortunately, since she wasn't a magician, Rambha had little to no interest in her. She was too busy inquiring where the Master Sorcerer was.

The deciding round of the obstacle race was in progress, with the finals of the equestrian events still to come. It would be an hour at least, perhaps two, before she could go back to the palace and find out—

Someone ran into the royal box.

Someone ran *urgently* into the royal box and whispered to the Maharaja.

Vasundhara's stomach tightened. Something had happened—something had gone wrong—she had *known* she should simply have taken charge of the Fire of the East herself instead of trusting a complicated plan devised by magicians—

The crowd cheered. The judges conferred. One of them stepped forward to announce the winner.

The Maharaja got to his feet and signalled to the trumpeters. Fanfare broke out around the arena, ending only when the spectators had fallen completely silent.

'Unfortunately, we will have to call a temporary halt to the events scheduled for this afternoon. There has been a minor . . . . ah . . . snag, which we are working on resolving. We encourage you to use this time to go home, refresh yourselves, enjoy the sights of our city, and return tomorrow morning, at which time we expect to resume. We will use the scheduled rest day the day after tomorrow to complete whatever remains of today's events. Thank you.'

Vasundhara transferred her gaze from her grandfather to Rambha.

Rambha looked *furious*.

Vasundhara barely stopped to watch the competitors go before hurrying to her grandfather and Rambha.

'What's happened?' she asked anxiously. 'Is it—' She stopped herself and looked at Rambha.

'There's been a problem,' the Maharaja said, trying to sound calm, but failing in the face of Rambha's icy glare. Vasundhara didn't blame him.

'I *knew* it,' Rambha said. 'I *knew* mortals couldn't be trusted. I *knew* it was only a matter of time—'

'Let's go to the palace,' the Maharaja said, clearly aware of the eyes of diplomats from most of the Free Lands on them. If Pür were the cause of the Inter-Realm Accord coming to an end, it would put him in an awkward position with his peers. 'We can speak there.'

'Yes, we'd better. And, of *course*, there's nobody to open a portal for us, because the magicians are all at the palace.'

'I can call one of the court magicians,' the Maharaja said.

'No. Let's just walk.'

Rambha set a brisk pace across the lawn. Vasundhara practically had to run to keep up.

'Idiocy,' Rambha muttered. 'Sheer, rank stupidity. It's partly my fault. I should have known better. Mortals are too emotional—too overconfident—and *Ravi*. It's his fault, really. He had *better* hope he gets killed because if I get him alive I will make him *rue* the day he was born. Falling in love with a mortal! He should know better.'

Vasundhara was torn between wanting to defend herself and Ravi and wanting to avoid being noticed by the Chief of the Celestial Dancers while she was in a bad mood.

Fortunately, Rambha wasn't interested in a response. Before the need for further conversation arose, they had arrived at the palace.

Everyone was gathered in the same antechamber—Vasundhara supposed they still ought to keep some degree of secrecy. There was no need to cause a general panic.

The door burst open as Rambha reached it—magic, or just the force of her anger, Vasundhara didn't know.

'What were you all *thinking*?' Rambha said, her expression ferocious enough to stop a Yaksha in his tracks. '*You*,' she said to the Minister for Inter-Realm Affairs. 'I *warned* you—you *promised* me—and Nalini—and *where* is the Master Sorcerer?'

'Here I am,' said Paras. The steel in his tone made Vasundhara acutely aware of why, exactly, he was the Master Sorcerer. It did occasionally happen that the person filling that role was meek and unprepossessing, but that wasn't the case with Paras. He was as prepossessing as they came; if a newcomer had been introduced to the room and asked to pick the Master Sorcerer, that newcomer, nine times out of ten, would unerringly choose Paras. (The tenth time, in an attempt to be clever, he might choose Asamanjas, who was several inches shorter than his brother.)

Paras faced Rambha now, without seeming at all intimidated.

'Would you care to explain to me,' snarled Rambha, '*why*, exactly, you—the Master Sorcerer, the most senior magician of the Mortal Realm—condoned this madness? Don't pretend it happened without your consent. You *must* have known.'

'I don't intend to pretend any such thing,' Paras said with dignity. 'We did what we had to do to recover the Sprite. I agree the event has been unfortunate, but—'

'I *told* you, if it came to that, to *let* the Sprite deal with the consequences of his stupidity. He should have known better than to get involved with a mortal. This is a violation of the Inter-Realm Accord—'

'Exigent circumstances,' Nalini said. '*And* not a single magician laid hands on the Fire of the East until it was stolen. Non-magicians aren't covered by the Accord. In any case, as I said, there's an exception for exigent circumstances.'

'You can't call this exigent when I *told* you the Inter-Realm was willing to make the sacrifice—'

'You *told* us?' Paras said, suddenly as angry as Rambha. 'Yes, *you* told *us*. And what about everyone in the Inter-Realm? What about the Sprites who have been *pouring* into Rajgir? Did you tell *them*? Or did you just think that the destruction caused to Rajgir by a lot of angry Sprites seeking vengeance for one of their own would be *our* problem?'

'I wouldn't have allowed any destruction!'

'You wouldn't have allowed it? You can't even make them go home! Your inability to control your own people left us no option but to look for the gem. You can choose to be *sensible* and accept it, and we'll keep things quiet and get it *back*. If you won't . . . then, in order to avoid disastrous consequences for all involved, we'll have to tell the Sprites in Rajgir, now, that Rambha was willing to let one of their number die.'

'Are you *threatening* me?'

'Yes,' Paras said simply.

'The Sprites *know* that we don't offer protection to those who get involved with mortals, especially when dangerous magic is involved,' Rambha said, but she suddenly sounded less sure of herself than she had a moment earlier.

'You would know best about that,' Paras said.

Rambha scowled. It made her look no less lovely. 'Very well. If you manage to get both the Fire of the East and the Sprite back, I will overlook this incident.'

'Good. I'm glad we're in agreement.'

'What do you need from me?'

'The magical output trackers in the Inter-Realm. We need details of blips, however small.'

'You'll have them in half an hour,' Rambha said and swept out of the room.

'What about Ravi?' Vasundhara burst out once she had gone, unable to restrain herself any longer. 'The kidnapper wanted the gem at noon.'

'The kidnapper never came. So we must assume that either the kidnapper was the one who took the Fire of the East, or the kidnapper knew that it was taken. There was no other reason for them not to show up.'

'Maybe the large crowd of waiting magicians,' Vasundhara suggested.

'Oh, no, we scrapped that. Without the real Fire of the East, there was no need to have so many magicians standing by. Still, nobody came.'

Rati was trying to be indignant. She *ought* to be indignant. It was bad enough to be in this uncouth country where magic could be practised in public and amulets sold at street corners like hemlock. But it was *insufferable* to be called to the palace by a ruler who could barely even keep his own *court* in order, leave alone the magicians nominally under his jurisdiction, and asked, like a child, whether she had been *indiscreet*.

'Certainly *not*,' she said coldly, in response to the Maharaja's question. 'I said nothing to anybody except Abhinav. In *Melucha*, we know the meaning of silence.'

The Maharaja looked at her hard.

'I'm told you don't like Kalban,' he said, changing tack with all the finesse of a sledgehammer.

Rati refrained, with difficulty, from rolling her eyes. 'I don't see what that has to do with anything. But, since you ask, I have nothing against Kalban personally. I just don't think he's as suitable to be the ruler of Melucha as his brother.'

'Some people would call that treason.'

Shel, who had accompanied Rati, looked at the Maharaja with well-bred surprise. 'In Melucha, we welcome the views of the Privy Council on all matters related to governance. As you do in Pür, I assume. If I remember correctly, you were thirty-eighth in line to the throne in your youth, yet for over forty years you have been one of the country's ablest rulers. That suggests either an *extraordinary* coincidence, or that somebody in Pür—possibly you, yourself—was of the view that the *first* in line for the throne wasn't best suited to the position. Or the second, or the third, or . . . I won't belabour the point. We understand each other.'

'We are not,' interjected the Maharani, 'trying to lay blame. But the Fire of the East is at large, and I have no doubt that members of the Meluchan court are aware of the dangers that might arise from such a powerful magical object being in the wrong hands. If you *do* have any information, you have my word that the source will not be disclosed to anyone outside this room.'

'Can you really make that promise?' Shel asked dryly.

'I *am* the Maharaja of Pür!' snapped the Maharaja. 'My word is law.'

'I see.'

'Also,' said the Maharani, 'Paras won't really care, Asamanjas has enough to deal with in Madh without taking on additional problems, Nalini and Kamakshi are both extremely practical in these things, and . . . the members of court know that Princess Persis has been helpful. That's all they need to know.'

'I wish I could help you,' Shel said, sounding truly regretful. 'But I know nothing.'

The Maharani turned to Rati.

This time Rati did roll her eyes. 'I didn't take the Fire of the East. I didn't *tell* anyone about the Fire of the East. I did tell Abhinav to accompany Kalban and Meenakshi if he could. I'm not blind, you know. Kalban has a distinct advantage in dealing with magicians—an advantage whose importance to international relations cannot be overlooked. I hoped Abhinav might . . . benefit. But that's all I did. I don't want to see a powerful magical object fall into the wrong hands any more than you do.'

The Maharani sighed. 'All right, thank you. We'll have you escorted back.'

'We can find our way without an escort,' said Shel.

'I daresay, but you're getting one. I promised Persis I'd arrange it. I don't want to try her temper at the moment, as I'm sure you can appreciate. She's angry enough about not being in time to find the Sprite at Lord Das's country home.'

Rati, about to get to her feet, stopped and looked at the Maharani. 'That's true, then? Lord Das *was* involved? Kalban told me he was *suspected.*'

'Oh, yes,' the Maharani said. 'At least . . . I wouldn't go so far as to say he was involved, not *willingly*. He claims, and I'm inclined to believe him, that he was blackmailed into it. Something about the source of some treasure he found—'

'*My* treasure,' muttered the Maharaja. 'He managed to keep it quiet that he got it off *my* land. We know the truth now. Unfortunately, the man's been promised immunity so I can't get the treasure from him.'

'Far be it from me to tell you your business,' Shel said, 'but perhaps a more pertinent question is which members of court are likely to have had the information that Lord Das wanted to conceal. Have you made no attempt to identify the blackmailer?'

CHAPTER XIX

Asamanjas had occasionally had cause to regret that he was one of the few completely unmagical scions of a long line that had produced some of the most highly-regarded—or notorious, depending on your view of these things—magicians in the Free Lands. He had regretted it deeply in his youth, when, sibling-fashion, he would have given much for the ability to turn Paras into a grasshopper and trap him in a jar with a few leaves.

Since growing to adulthood, he had regretted it less. Madh was as full of unmagical people who wielded considerable influence as it was of magicians. Asamanjas attributed most of his good relations with the priests and merchants of the city to his inability to make it rain on them when there was a minor disagreement.

At the moment, however, he wished he could be doing something—*anything*, including scouring Rajgir for any trace of the Fire of the East—rather than poring over records of court correspondence going back three years.

The Maharani was with him. The Maharaja, Vasundhara and the Minister for Law and Order were preparing the City Guard to deal with the situation if the worst came to pass and the Sprites rioted. All the magicians were searching the city end to end for any trace of either the Fire of the East or the missing Sprite.

They hadn't found anything yet, or Asamanjas and the Maharani would have heard.

Asamanjas scowled as he saw yet *another* taxation report. He had come to Rajgir to attend Princess Vasundhara's swayamvara and enjoy a well-deserved holiday. Yet, here he was, dealing with more *paperwork*. He might as well have stayed in Madh.

'Look at this,' the Maharani said suddenly.

Asamanjas took the document she was holding out to him. It was a Magical Being Sighting report. Hundreds were filed in Madh every single day; the Dangerous Beings Control Squad kept them for three months and then used them for kindling.

'What about it?' he said.

'It's a Yakshini sighting. Look at the date. It's two years old.'

'There must have been thousands—*tens* of thousands of these reports that year. And hundreds, at least, involving Yakshas and Yakshinis.'

'It says it was investigated and found false,' said the Maharani. 'Look at the signature of the investigating officer.'

Asamanjas squinted. 'Bahuka. The Minister for Inter-Realm Affairs. I still don't see—wait. The *Minister* investigated this himself? When you say the rest of Pür has fewer sightings than Madh—'

'Fewer, yes, but still enough that it would be unusual for the Minister for Inter-Realm Affairs to investigate one himself. That would only happen if it were . . . important, for some reason, in which case it would have been brought to the attention of the Maharaja . . . '

'And it would be in the court record,' finished Asamanjas. 'Is it in the court record?'

'I've seen no sign of it. Leave all the rest of that, let's look at the documents from the Minister for Inter-Realm Affairs.'

⚔

Chitralekha got to her feet.

She had spent at least an hour staring at the readouts from the Inter-Realm Sensors. If Celestial Dancers were capable of getting headaches, she would have had one by now.

'What are you doing?' snapped Gopali, who was helping her. 'We're not finished.'

'We're not going to find anything. Every bit of significant magical output today can be accounted for. Meenakshi getting us out of the tunnel, it's been fairly quiet since then. The Master of the Royal Academy and the Minister for Inter-Realm Affairs, turning the fake gem into a magical object. Other than that, there are just intermittent minor bursts—nothing you don't see every day. Even the Master Sorcerer has been too busy. His readings are below normal.'

'That'll be Meenakshi,' Gopali said, as light flashed in the study. 'I hope she's got good news.'

But Meenakshi, when she entered the room, had no news of any sort. Wherever the Fire of the East was, it wasn't within Rajgir's city limits.

'Have you found anything in the readouts?' she asked.

'I can't see anything unusual.' Chitralekha gestured at the hundreds of long slips of paper spread on the table before her. 'This is every magician known or suspected to be in Rajgir today. There's nothing suspicious. The only spikes are you, the Master of the Royal Academy and the Minister for Inter-Realm Affairs, and we know the causes of those.'

'Hmmm,' Meenakshi murmured. 'We'd better find it quickly. Then maybe Kalban will stop making direful predictions.'

She looked over the slips of paper. Chitralekha doubted she'd find anything. Most of them showed very little magical output, especially in the afternoon, once people had realized—

Meenakshi made a soft noise.

'What?' Gopali asked, sudden hope in her voice, evidently recognizing the sound. 'Do you see anything?'

'Whose is that?'

'This?' Chitralekha picked up the one Meenakshi had pointed at. 'Dikaiopolis. The Yaunic Ambassador. But there's nothing wrong with it. He's had barely any magical activity—well below his normal output—'

'Yes, but look at this.' Meenakshi indicated the output for that morning, which was a flat line just barely above the axis.

'Oh—yes—you do see that pattern sometimes when a magician's been . . . ' Chitralekha trailed off. 'Oh, so *that's* what it was. I never thought of that. I was looking for spikes.'

'What was it?' Gopali asked. 'What pattern?'

'A straight line,' Meenakshi said. 'My guess is that's what you see when a magician's trying to maintain a steady stream of magic for an experiment of some sort . . . which the Yaunic Ambassador should have had no reason to do, when he was supposed to have been representing the Tyrant at the swayamvara of Princess Vasundhara.'

'I see what you mean, but I don't know that this is enough output to mean anything,' Chitralekha said. 'The Fire of the East would lead to a larger spike than that, surely.'

'Not if he was just trickling a little magic into it to see if it worked.' Meenakshi picked up the readout and took it to the window. 'I'll take a closer look at this. Where's the Yaunic Ambassador?'

'I'll find out,' said Gopali, hurtling from the room. 'Chitralekha, tell Rambha. Meenakshi, figure out how you're going to get the Fire of the East off him if he has it.'

$$\maltese$$

Chitralekha, mumbling something about finding Rambha, left.

Meenakshi studied the readout in silent solitude.

Socially inept Meenakshi might be, her ability to read non-verbal cues might be dismal, but she could think logically.

The Yaunic Ambassador might *have* the Fire of the East, but he couldn't possibly have taken it from the vault himself. He hadn't been in the room with them. Either way, he would have been noticed entering the palace. Someone else *must* have been involved—someone who had been *in* the room—

Meenakshi paused.

Someone who had caused a diversion, but who wouldn't have needed to use magic, because he could physically handle the stone—

Someone who had been sitting right beside the Minister for Law and Order—

Light flashed in the study.

'There's *nothing*,' Kalban came into the room, looking like the High Priest of the Sun God was harassing him for a tax concession. 'Nothing *anywhere*. And you don't look worried,' he added. 'Why don't you look worried? Have you found something?'

'It's the Yaunic Ambassador,' Meenakshi said. 'Gopali's gone to find out where he is. He isn't in Rajgir, I'm sure. We've searched the city. The question is where he would have gone. He couldn't have gone back to Yauna with the Fire of the East. The Tyrant would chain him to a cliff to be eaten by a sea monster.'

The Tyrant of Yauna took a dim view of magicians breaking the terms of the Inter-Realm Accord.

'He was talking to *you* rather a lot at all the events,' Kalban said. 'What was he saying?'

'Oh—nothing, really—asking about my studies—he was interested in the new Alchemy lab at the Academy. And he was cheering for the contenders from Vraja.'

'The sort of chaos that would come to Pür if one of those magic-fearing lunatics were to be consort is exactly what Yauna wants. I can understand why the Tyrant-in-waiting didn't come to the swayamvara . . . The Ambassador was interested in the Alchemy lab, was he?'

'Most people are interested in the Alchemy lab . . . most *sensible* people.'

'Yes, but Yaunic magicians don't usually study at the Academy. They have their own school. I don't see why the Alchemy lab should particularly interest him, and he *couldn't* use the Fire of the East . . . and keep it secret . . . '

'You're thinking he'd go to Madh?'

'Eventually, I think that's his plan, but he couldn't have gone *yet*. The Maharaja ordered that all portals be monitored since we brought the stone into the city. If the Ambassador had to hide somewhere and wait for things to settle down . . . it would have to be somewhere he could reach without a portal, on foot or by horse.'

'Are you thinking . . . '

'Lord Das's house? Let's go there.'

'As soon as Chitralekha's back,' Meenakshi said. 'I promised I'd tell her.'

༶

'There's no getting around it. The trail goes back to the Minister for Inter-Realm Affairs.' Asamanjas put down the last letter. 'It all makes sense. We should have seen it sooner. Who *else* would know that Ravi was serious enough about marrying Vasundhara that he'd want to participate in the swayamvara? Who would Ravi come to when he wasn't sure where to stay because protocol forbade him from staying in the palace and Rambha wouldn't let him stay at the Inter-Realm Embassy? Who would know exactly how Rambha would react to the ransom demand, necessitating a clandestine retrieval of the Fire of the East? We should have realized it.'

'Now we have confirmation.' The Maharani sighed. 'I still don't understand why he'd want to kidnap a Sprite and steal a forbidden magical object. What could he hope to gain by it?'

'What could a magician hope to gain from the Fire of the East?' Asamanjas asked dryly.

'The most powerful magicians in the Free Lands are in Pür. Soon, they'll all know what he's done. Fire of the East or not, the Minister for Inter-Realm Affairs can't hope to last against them.'

'Maybe,' said a new voice, 'he didn't intend to stay in Pür.'

Asamanjas snatched at the nearest heavy object—a candlestick—and raised it in self-defence before he saw that the newcomer was Rambha, accompanied by Chitralekha. Although Asamanjas had been informed of Chitralekha's presence in Rajgir, he hadn't encountered her thus far. He groaned at the sight of her.

'Why is it that whenever there's trouble, it's always *you*?'

'Just your good fortune, I suppose,' Chitralekha said brightly. 'We looked at the readouts. I won't bore you with the details, but the Yaunic Ambassador has the Fire of the East. We've tracked him to Lord Das's house—he was seen by one of the City Guard. Meenakshi and Kalban have gone to get it. They're going to hold off on actually entering the estate until somebody has eyes on the Sprite. Rati was trying to tell Abhinav to go with them, but for once he showed some good sense and said he'd stay out of a magical fight. You might want to talk to the Prince of Melucha about reining in the members of his Privy Council. They interfere far too much.'

'Never mind Abhinav,' Asamanjas said impatiently. 'Why didn't Paras go with them?'

'He will,' Rambha said, 'if he's *needed*. I would prefer to keep the Master Sorcerer away from a Forbidden Magical Artefact until his assistance becomes absolutely necessary. If a magician *must* handle the Fire of the East, better it's one who isn't yet Licensed. Less paperwork.' Rambha shrugged. 'If the Master Sorcerer's probable successor is everything I've been led to believe, I daresay she'll manage. It's a good test of her mettle.' Asamanjas could scarcely credit the change that had come over Rambha in a few hours. 'In the meantime, are you *certain* about the Minister for Inter-Realm Affairs?'

'As certain as we can be. We don't know *why* he would have wanted the gem. He couldn't hope to stay in Pür after kidnapping a Sprite. Yauna wouldn't harbour him either, if he was in possession of the Fire of the East. If anything, the Tyrant is *less* understanding of magicians' quirks than the Maharaja. He wouldn't take in a fugitive.'

'We'll get those details from him,' Rambha said, with calm implacability. 'Never fret. He'll tell us everything. But first, we need to find the Sprite. If the Minister for Inter-Realm Affairs is the kidnapper, where might he keep the Sprite? Nalini told me there was somebody in the Inter-Realm Liaison Bureau in Rajgir she was investigating who might—' She broke off as somebody knocked. 'That must be her now.'

Rambha opened the door to a young woman.

'You wanted to speak to me?' the woman said.

'Are you Mitra?'

'Yes.' Mitra entered the room and shut the door behind her. 'And I know that Nalini has been having me investigated. And before you ask, *yes*, I delivered the letter from the Minister and I put it next to you though I knew you weren't Vasundhara. I thought, if you knew what he planned, you'd prevent it from happening.'

'Why not just tell someone, if you knew?' the Maharani said sharply.

'Because he threatened to ruin me if I wouldn't help him!' Mitra snapped. 'He said he'd have *me* blamed for everything, and who was going to take my word over the Minister's? I had a hard enough time convincing him that I accidentally mistook Rambha for Princess Vasundhara. It was fortunate she was seated where she was and I could claim to have seen her only from behind.'

'I like this one,' Rambha proclaimed. 'She shows initiative. Do you have any idea where the Minister for Inter-Realm Affairs would have taken the Sprite?'

'He said there's a disused temple somewhere—I don't know exactly where but it's far away.'

'The Minister for Inter-Realm Affairs handled the Sighting report himself,' the Maharani said. 'So he knew exactly where to find the Yakshini's cave.'

Chitralekha drew in a sharp breath. 'Do you think he could have worked backwards to find the statue of the Goddess of Speech in the desert?'

'I suppose so,' Asamanjas said. 'It's been—what, two years?— since Lord Das found the treasure. You don't think the Sprite's being kept prisoner in the middle of the desert?'

'There would usually be a temple attached to the statue,' Chitralekha said. 'Especially one in the desert, built in the days before magicians discovered how to make Mortal Realm portals—a place for travellers to rest—'

'But if it was buried underground—'

'Under sand, but the inside of the temple may have been intact. Sprites don't need air. The Summoner could have put in an air hole for himself.'

'You went through the cave *and* the tunnel and you saw the statue. You would have seen some sign of the Sprite.'

'We didn't have time. Kalban was hurrying us back. And—this is the thing—Meenakshi *said* she sensed something wrong. Kalban didn't want to take the time to stop and investigate—'

'I wish he had done,' muttered Asamanjas.

'I'll send someone to tell Nalini,' said the Maharani. 'She and Kamakshi and Persis can go to this statue. Do you know where it is?' she asked Chitralekha. 'They'll need someone to give them directions to open the portal.'

'I can show them,' Rambha said. 'I was there when the statue was put up. I want to be present to see the Sprite and the magicians concerned.'

Asamanjas didn't know whether it was the Sprite or the magicians who ought to be more afraid.

Chapter XX

A glowing line of light appeared in the starlit darkness of the desert. It lengthened. Space seemed to turn sideways as it opened into a circle.

Nalini was first through. She waited for everyone else to follow before she closed the portal. The sudden darkness that fell seemed absolute for a moment; then her eyes adjusted.

Something large blotted out the stars before her.

Nalini raised her hands. Faint light glowed on the head of what, if it was uncovered intact, would be an enormous statue. Nalini felt a sudden chill; if it was uncovered, in this place from which she had once watched over caravans trudging across the Kos Desert, the Goddess of Speech must have enormous power.

'Fan out,' she said, keeping her voice low, just in case. 'Watch out for Meenakshi's staircase—we don't need anyone tumbling down it. No magical flares. We don't want to alert whoever is inside.' Or, she added silently to herself, draw any *other* attention. 'If you find something, hoot like an owl.'

'I can't *hoot* like an *owl*,' said the Master of the Academy. His voice was loud in the silence of the night. Nalini thought the statue's eyes flashed. 'I'm one of the leading scholars of Madh, not a bird-imitator at a country fair.'

'Quieter,' Nalini hissed. 'Can you whistle?'

The Master of the Academy puckered his lips. No sound came out.

'I'll stay with him,' Chitralekha said. 'I can whistle.'

'All right. Keep your voices down, everyone. Do you know the plan? The first priority is to get the Sprite out safely. As soon as we're assured of that, I'll open a portal to the road outside Lord Das's estate in Rajgir. Chitralekha will go and tell Meenakshi and Kalban they can move in. Persis, if we don't need her here, will go with her to help them.'

Everyone scattered, soon visible only as faint points of light in the darkness.

Nalini stayed where she was, meeting the eyes of the statue. They glowed faintly orange—possibly they were made of fire agates as well. She knew there was no real reason to be afraid—the Goddess of Speech wasn't exactly a *kindly* goddess, but she was known to be just. All the same . . .

The statue must be *big*. Amsuman's will had said it was five times as tall as a man. Either he had known some extraordinarily tall men, or he had understated. From the size of the head, it must be at least twice that height . . .

Unless it was a seated statue. That was possible.

Did it matter?

She heard someone call out in the distance. One of the guards, perhaps.

A seated statue this size might be hollow inside.

The temple didn't have to be *huge*, and it probably *hadn't* been, or it would show up on ancient records.

She turned to Rambha, who was standing behind her.

'You *must* have known, the moment the statue was mentioned! Are you going to tell us how to get in, or do we need to waste time looking for a door?'

Rambha smiled. 'From what I recall, the door seems to be buried several feet deep in sand. But if you go down the stairs Meenakshi made, there might be a way in from underneath.'

The horses were tethered to a tree. Kalban had remembered to bring adequately supplied nosebags, so they were, for the most part, quiet, the occasional whicker or twig snapped underhoof not being worth mentioning.

He was certain, all the same, that their presence hadn't gone unnoticed.

Three times a guard had come up to the gate, looked outside, and gone away again.

When he pointed this out to Meenakshi, she only shrugged and said that they had put a magical perimeter around the place so nobody could open a portal; it was a new building whose architect had promised them, on pain of being handed over to Rambha if he lied, that there were no secret passages in or out past the boundary wall; and anyway she could sense the Fire of the East inside.

Kalban could sense it too.

He didn't know how they were going to relieve the Yaunic Ambassador of it. That sort of thing was usually Meenakshi's job. Kalban just had to get them *into* the room without the Yaunic Ambassador escaping first.

'Did you want to take it from Abhinav?' he asked softly, eyes on the lights that shone from the windows.

'What, the Fire of the East?'

'Yes.'

Meenakshi laughed. 'Didn't you? It *would* have been *interesting* to see just what it *could* do.'

'*Meenakshi*,' Kalban protested, scandalized, although he should have known better than to ask. 'You can't just say you wanted to experiment with a Class V Artefact!'

'Why else would anyone want it? Oh, yes, I know for nefarious evil purposes,' Meenakshi said quickly, when Kalban glared at her. 'I didn't mean *that*. The Yaunic Ambassador has had it for hours and he's not done anything awful.'

'I wonder why he took it. He's not powerful enough to last long with it—he must know *that*. Didn't he say *anything* in all the time he was talking to you?'

'Oh, yes, he talked a *lot*. I didn't listen much.'

'That would have been *far* too sensible.'

'I didn't know he was going to steal the Fire of the East! Anyway, it wasn't very interesting. He was just droning on and *on* about the difficulties of his position—and how he hoped Vraja would win, he talked a lot about that—'

'The difficulties of his position,' Kalban repeated. 'As Ambassador? And you said he wanted to talk to you about the new Alchemy lab . . . Do they have anything there that he couldn't get in Rajgir or Yauna?'

'I don't know what they have in Yauna. The new lab in Madh has stable facilities for the creation of magical objects that are better than any lab in Rajgir . . . Actually, that would be a good place to experiment with the Fire of the East, if one wanted to. The rooms are fully magically sealed. But how would that help? He couldn't stay in the facility forever.'

'If the Fire of the East were found in the new Alchemy lab, people would assume the Chair of Alchemy had something to do with it. Or perhaps even the Master of the Academy. They might be accused of kidnapping the Sprite, too. That would discredit the Academy, and Madh by extension.'

'Is discrediting the Academy enough motive for this?'

'Discrediting the Academy—*and* disrupting the swayamvara. Do you think Vasundhara would actually have agreed to marry somebody else?' Deciding he didn't want to hear Meenakshi's views on that, Kalban answered the question himself, '*Eventually* she might, but right now? In . . . two and a half days? She would have refused.'

'Then what would happen to whoever won the swayamvara? I suppose she could say she didn't choose anyone and so nobody won.'

'She would mortally offend every other country. She would then be left, assuming she *did* want to do her duty by her royal line at some point in the future, with very few options . . . like the Tyrant-in-waiting of Yauna, who didn't come at all. Or some minor lord from Pür—Meenakshi!' Kalban hissed, clutching at her arm. 'He's the Maharaja's cousin!'

'Who? The Tyrant-in-waiting? How do you know?'

'Not the Tyrant-in-waiting! The Minister for Inter-Realm Affairs. You *said* he might have something to do with it.'

'He's married already.'

'He has a son. Only eighteen now, but in a year or two . . . when Vasundhara had mourned and was ready to marry . . . And if the Minister and the Yaunic Ambassador were in it together, that would give the Tyrant of Yauna influence in Pür . . . Either way, Yauna would be stronger. And if the Academy had been discredited . . . '

'Most of the leading magicians of Pür and the rest of the Free Lands would go to Yauna. Making Yauna even more powerful. You don't think the Tyrant had something to do with this?'

'I think we can't do anything about it even if he did. He's the ruler of a sovereign country. We can just *try* to prevent it from happening. As soon as Chitralekha tells us we can move in.'

⚔

'Remember, it's magically sealed,' Nalini said in a whisper. 'They can't open a portal to the outside—so all we have to do is make sure they don't leave *physically*. First priority, see that the Sprite is safe. Take down Bahuka first—he's the greater threat—and then the Summoner. Guards, stay *back* until the magicians are subdued. Ready?'

There were various sounds of assent.

Nalini nodded to two of the guards, who were standing next to a section of wall Rambha had pointed out to them. It was still partially submerged, as a result of Meenakshi's earlier efforts, although the water had receded considerably and would probably be down to a trickle again by the following morning.

Each of the guards grasped an iron ring in the wall. They heaved with all their might.

A block slid out of the wall a few inches.

The guards were replaced by another pair, who heaved the block out further, and then a third, who pulled it all the way out of the wall and dropped it with a splash into the water.

The opening would admit one person at a time.

Nalini went first, followed by the Master of the Academy, Persis, Kamakshi, Rambha and Chitralekha, and finally the guards. She found herself in a tunnel sloping gently upwards. Yellow light glimmered at the end.

Nalini went up as quickly as she could without falling on the slippery wet stone. The tunnel widened halfway to the end. The Master of the Academy came up beside her.

'You break the spell holding the Sprite,' he said in an undertone. 'The rest of us will deal with the magicians.'

Nalini nodded. She could sense a Summoning spell—weak enough that it must be the Summoning Service agent holding it, not the Minister. That was good. It would be easier to break. But it also meant the Minister was free to attack.

'Don't worry,' Persis said, as though sensing her thoughts. 'We'll deal with him.'

A shadow appeared in the light at the end of the tunnel.

'*Duck!*' Nalini called.

Everyone threw themselves down at once—including the Master of the Academy. Scholars in Madh needed good reflexes.

Something whooshed above them. There was a crash in the tunnel behind them.

'Oh, that's *it*,' hissed Kamakshi, scrambling to her feet, Persis with her. 'I am *done*.'

Light flashed overhead.

⚜

The Master Sorcerer had an enviable ability to compartmentalize.

His position precluded him from direct involvement in a magical fight until it became necessary for the sake of the greater good to separate the belligerents. He thought it was a foolish rule, personally, since it usually meant that by the time he *became* involved, matters had progressed to an unfortunate pass. But it had been the rule for generations—for four generations, to be precise, ever since Paras's great-great grandmother had put an end to a street fight by turning the combatants (and, since she had had an unfortunate tendency to use a metaphorical sledgehammer where a needle would do, about four dozen onlookers) into toads. It had taken the City Guard hours to round them all up and there had been reports of people eating flies for months.

Or so Paras had heard.

Since he couldn't be present to retrieve either the Sprite or the Fire of the East, there was little point worrying about either. His wife and daughter were more than capable, Nalini, Persis and Kalban were accomplished magicians, and the charlatan of the Academy could, at least, do no real harm. Paras might as well concentrate on his research.

He made valiant efforts in that direction. Unfortunately, his brother didn't share his rational outlook and insisted on breaking into his concentration with remarks like, 'How can you *read* at a time like this?' and, 'Have you *considered* how wrong this could go?'

'You should have gone with them,' Paras said, after the fifth such interruption, 'if you were just going to worry about it. *Some* of us are trying to read.'

'I *wanted* to go with them, but Persis's son—the *other* one, not Kalban—was just *looking* for an excuse to be allowed to go and she would have been furious with me if I'd given him one by going myself.'

'If you're going to worry about what'll make Persis furious, you won't be able to do anything. Why don't you read a book? There's that history of Inter-Realm relations you ordered last month and I *know* you've not read it yet.'

'Read *history*,' Asamanjas said bitterly. 'Read history at a time like *this*? Trust you to do that!'

'I suppose you think the logical course of action is to fret about things you can't help at a time like this?'

Asamanjas threw up his hands and began pacing up and down the room. Paras considered going to another empty antechamber, but his brother would only follow him there.

There were voices outside. Asamanjas went to the window and looked out.

'It's the Prince of Melucha and his son,' he reported, although Paras had expressed no interest.

Paras scowled. 'Is *nobody* capable of reading quietly? And if they aren't capable of reading quietly, they have the Embassy of Melucha that's *full* of people to disturb. Why must they come and bother *me*?'

'Also two Dancers,' Asamanjas went on.

'If they ask for me, tell them I've gone back to Madh.'

Naturally, Asmanjas did no such thing. The Celestial Dancers were shown in first. They were carrying a box between them—a box that seemed too small to need two people to carry it. They deposited it on the table.

'Shield box for magical artefacts,' said one of the Dancers. 'Rambha sent for one but it's taken us some time to organize it.'

'Inefficient,' Asamanjas sniffed. 'It's been *hours* since she asked for it. Why the delay? Isn't this your *job*?'

'There aren't many shield boxes capable of holding a Class V Forbidden Magical Artefact. We don't have them just sitting *around*,' said one of the Dancers. 'Where is the artefact?'

'It's being retrieved now. It's on an estate just outside the city.'

'We would prefer that it wasn't carried through the city unshielded,' said the Dancer. 'There would be too much risk of an attack. Can you send this to the magicians retrieving the artefact?'

Paras frowned. 'I'm not supposed to go there, but—'

'I'll take it,' said a new voice from the doorway.

Paras looked incredulously at the Prince Regnant of Melucha and his younger son.

'Summon the Sprite as soon as I break the spell,' Nalini hissed. 'He can't dematerialize from here. Summon him and get him *out*.'

The Master of the Academy nodded. Scholars in Madh who were capable of Summoning learnt to do it quickly and efficiently, under difficult circumstances. Especially, scholars who had a habit of maintaining running feuds with other magicians.

'On my signal!' Nalini snapped.

CHAPTER XXI

'It's a nice evening,' the Prince Regnant of Melucha said pleasantly, opening an Alchemy guide. 'I see you have some unusual literature here. My son has often spoken of the libraries of Madh and their rare volumes.'

Paras, who had now given up on doing his research—Asmanjas wouldn't let him hear the *end* of it if he ignored a visiting head of state in order to read, however unexpected or unwelcome the visit—made a non-committal noise.

Asamanjas, on the other hand, said incredulously, 'You let your son *go*?'

'Why is it that whenever *I* ask people questions in that tone, you tell me about the importance of maintaining good diplomatic relations?' Paras demanded.

'Because when *you* ask people questions in that tone, you're usually implying that they're idiots.'

'In fairness to the Master Sorcerer,' said the Prince Regnant of Melucha, turning a page, 'I think your implication was the same, Lord Asmanajas. What an interesting picture.'

Paras, despite himself, leaned over to look. 'It's a warning,' he said, 'not to overload magic.'

'We've known your wife since she came to the Royal Academy as a twelve-year-old,' Asamanjas said. 'There's no need to be so formal. And since you bring up the subject, yes, I *was* implying, not without justification, that you're an idiot.'

'You let your niece go.'

'My niece can be foolish and impulsive, but she *is* a powerful magician. It's likely that she will one day be the senior magician of Madh and the rest of the Free Lands. She needs training in dealing with these situations. It will eventually be her responsibility.'

'I applaud your logic. And my younger son, although not a magician, may also find himself dealing with a similar situation one day, given who his mother and brother are. He needs training in being present at a magical fight without getting caught in the crossfire.'

'Quite a sensible attitude,' said Paras. 'That must be why Persis likes you.'

'Lunatics,' muttered Asmanajas. 'All *lunatics*.'

Kalban was *tired* of waiting, and he was tempted to move in—surely the others must have retrieved the Sprite by *now*—when he heard a sound that filled him with annoyance.

Hoofbeats on the road. A single rider, coming from the direction of the city.

Who could possibly be fool enough to travel out of Rajgir, *alone*, in the middle of a magical emergency? The last thing they needed was to have some unwary idiot caught in the middle of this.

He peered into the road. The moon was out and nearly full, so he had a clear view of the rider.

It was Abhinav.

Kalban should have known.

'Oh, no, he *doesn't*,' he said furiously, stepping out into the road.

Abhinav saw him and drew rein.

'What are you *doing*?' Kalban snapped. 'I thought you were told to stay in the city! Get off the road. Someone's going to see you.'

Abhinav leapt off his horse and led it to the side. He tethered it next to Kalban's and Meenakshi's, before he opened the pannier and took out a box.

'The Master Sorcerer told me to give this to you. It's to hold the Fire of the East when you bring it back, so every magician in the city doesn't realize you have it. Apparently, there are rumours spreading, and someone unscrupulous might attempt to waylay you as you return to the palace with it.' Abhinav shrugged. 'I'm sure you know that better than I do.'

'*Father* asked you to bring us this?' Meenakshi said doubtfully.

'*Someone* had to bring it. He couldn't come himself. I happened to be there and, naturally, I volunteered—'

'I suppose it's a waste of time expecting you to go back,' Kalban growled. 'We don't have time to argue anyway. We'll be going in at any moment. Just try to stay *out* of the way.'

The spell broke in a cascade of white light.

'Now!' said Nalini. 'Now, now, *now*! Hurry *up*, man!'

The Master of the Academy, more accustomed to being the hurrier than the hurried, glared at her. A moment later, the Sprite wavered and then steadied in the Summoning circle in the middle of the room.

'Come *here*!' said the Master of the Academy. '*Now!*'

Not needing to be told twice, the Sprite ran across the room and got behind Nalini.

'No harm to any mortal,' the Master of the Academy said. 'No interference with the business of the Mortal Realm, no attempts to intimidate, threaten or—'

'I *know*!' the Sprite snapped irritably. 'I *am* engaged to Princess Vasundhara.'

'Not yet, you're not,' said Persis. 'And you won't be unless we can sort out this mess. Master, give him permission to go to Rajgir with Chitralekha.'

Kamakshi edged around Persis to stand next to Nalini and hold off their opponents.

'Whatever you're doing, do it *quickly*!' she said. 'Then we can focus on putting an end to this instead of worrying about the Sprite.'

'*Done*,' Persis opened a portal behind them. '*Master!*' The Master of the Academy nodded. 'Good enough. Chitralekha, take the Sprite and *go*. Leave him with the Master Sorcerer and ask him to open a portal for you to tell Kalban and Meenakshi to go in and get the Fire of the East.'

None too gently, Chitralekha seized Ravi by the arm and pulled him through the portal.

When the line of light appeared in the middle of the road, Kalban said, '*Finally!*'

'Can we go in?' Meenakshi demanded, before Chitralekha had even fully exited the portal. 'Did you get the Sprite?'

'He's safe with your father. Do you need to knock?'

'If by knock you mean magically open the gates,' Meenakshi said, starting up the road, 'then, yes, we're going to knock.'

The gates burst open as she reached them. She walked through, Kalban on her heels, Abhinav and Chitralekha following a careful ten paces behind.

Meenakshi didn't need to *search*. The Fire of the East wasn't *passive* now. It was being used—carefully, gently, yes, but even so its presence was far stronger than the thrum she had felt in the cave. Now it was *alive*.

Meenakshi could understand why Class V Magical Artefacts were forbidden.

She flung open doors until, in what looked like a library, she found the Yaunic Ambassador standing over a table, hands on the Fire of the East. Kalban and Chitralekha followed her into the room. Abhinav, with belated prudence, stayed outside.

'It's over, Ambassador,' Kalban said. 'The Sprite has been rescued. Your accomplices must have been captured by now. Give us the gem.'

Chitralekha said, 'Give us the Fire of the East, come peacefully, and I will personally tell Rambha you cooperated.'

The Yaunic Ambassador looked up, but his vacant eyes seemed to be gazing, not at them, but into a far distant future.

'The Celestial Dancers know everything.' Kalban sounded uneasy. 'Give us the Fire of the East.'

'Give you the Fire of the East.' The words were barely audible, almost a sigh.

Meenakshi tensed at the sound. Something had happened to the Ambassador.

'Do you know what happens,' he went on, still so softly she had to strain to hear, 'when a magical artefact lies forgotten in a cave for five hundred years, brooded over by a chained Yakshini, while people think and wonder what happened to it . . . and then slowly it turns into a legend, and they make up stories about it? Power builds up. Oh, yes. Power builds up.'

Chitralekha caught Meenakshi's arm before Meenakshi could move. The air shimmered, and Chitralekha was suddenly . . . different. Kalban shook his head as though trying to clear it. Even Meenakshi could feel Chitralekha's magic, different from that of any mortal, tugging at her senses.

'Give us the Fire of the East,' Chitralekha said. Her voice echoed through the room, bouncing off the walls, filling Meenakshi's hearing.

The Ambassador looked, for a moment, as though he would obey.

Then he tightened his grip on the stone.

Meenakshi felt a surge of *something*.

'*No*,' the Ambassador said coldly. 'I *won't* give you the gem. It's mine. You won't have it from me.'

'I *said*,' Chitralekha said more forcefully, her voice coming down like the sonic equivalent of a ton of bricks, '*give us the Fire of the East. Now.*'

'I . . . will . . . *not*.'

The sudden silence in the room rang like the pealing of a thousand bells.

'I can't do it,' Chitralekha gasped. 'With the Fire of the East, he's too strong. He can resist me. You're going to have to get it from him.'

Meenakshi stared at the Ambassador, trying to come up with a plan. Under normal circumstances, she'd be more than a match for him, especially with Kalban's help, but while he had the gem—

'We need a distraction,' she said under her breath.

'*That* I can provide.' Chitralekha backed out of the library.

'Ravi?' Vasundhara came into the room cautiously, as though not daring to believe her eyes. 'Ravi!' Asamanjas had the sense to avert his gaze in time. Paras didn't, and he suddenly went red and opened his book again.

'Ah, a happy ending,' the Prince Regnant of Melucha said. 'How uplifting.'

'Not yet, it isn't,' Asamanjas retorted. 'Vasundhara, if you've quite finished—'

'Oh—I'm so sorry. Of course.' Vasundhara went like quicksilver from being a young woman reuniting with her chosen suitor to being the future Maharani of Pür. 'We have more important things to do. What's happening?'

'We're expecting three criminals to be brought in at any moment. Unfortunately, because of the nature of the violation—stealing and using a forbidden magical artefact and kidnapping a Sprite—we'll have to let Rambha take them to the Inter-Realm to stand trial.'

'That's not a problem, is it? Is there anything I can do?'

'Not at the moment. One of them is Yaunic, but that's for your grandfather to worry about. There's nothing for us to do just now but wait. Do you have Lord Das in custody?'

'He's being held at the palace. Do you need information? That won't be a problem. He's willing to say *anything* and implicate anyone to avoid being handed over to the Celestial Dancers. The difficulty will be getting him to *stop* talking.'

'We'll probably want some explanations from him after this is over.'

Silence fell.

It was broken by Shel.

'Do you still intend to marry?' he asked Vasundhara and Ravi.

'Why wouldn't we?' said Vasundhara. 'After all this trouble? Ravi only needs to participate in *one* event of the swayamvara to qualify. There's still enough time—and I'm the *judge*. If I say the last event accounts for ninety-nine percent of the score, then it does. That's the *point*.'

'Naturally, naturally. You'll have to forgive the interference. I wonder if you've thought the matter through. A kidnapping attempt that has been made once might be made again. When you're Maharani, there will be more incentive and you will have more enemies.'

'There would be just as much incentive to kidnap Ravi if he were mortal.'

'Yes, there would. But kidnappers couldn't simply *Summon* him at will, and the kidnapping wouldn't lead to a potential Sprite uprising in the Mortal Realm. I'm not telling you what to do, Princess Vasundhara. I'm only advising you to *think*.'

'Go and tell Abhinav to go *straight* to my father if this doesn't work. Then come and help me.'

Kalban vanished, and reappeared a moment later.

'Abhinav's not there. I think he's gone to help Chitralekha with her *diversion*. It's his own fault if he gets himself killed. What do you need me to do?'

'Start collapsing the floor under him.'

'He'll only levitate himself.'

'That'll split his focus. I can get in and take the gem when Chitralekha's diversion happens.'

'Meenakshi,' Kalban said, 'what are you going to do?'

'Exactly what I promised.'

Rambha, looking at the two prisoners secured in magically sealed cells, smiled a satisfied smile.

'*That'll* keep the Sprites happy. Now all we need is the return of the Fire of the East, and we can put this unfortunate incident behind us.'

'It's not *quite* so simple as that,' said the Maharaja. 'What do you intend to do with the Yaunic Ambassador? These two you can have, and welcome,' he said, ignoring the alarmed reactions from the occupants of the cells. 'They're under my law. The Yaunic Ambassador has diplomatic immunity. I can't give him to you.'

'He has diplomatic immunity from the laws of Pür, not the Inter-Realm Accord. He's *mine*.'

'The Tyrant of Yauna was *very* unpleasant the last time we had to expel an Ambassador,' said the Maharaja.

'If I remember correctly, that was in your great-uncle's time, so surely it was a different Tyrant?'

'Besides,' said Asamanjas, 'I'm *sure* the Tyrant will be glad to allow his Ambassador to be tried in the Inter-Realm when he realizes that the alternative is for the Celestial Dancers to conduct a more thorough investigation in Yauna itself.'

The Maharaja brightened considerably. 'You're quite right. I'll write to him now.'

The door on the other side of the library opened.

The Yaunic Ambassador, intent on staying ahead of the flooring that Kalban was loosening and allowing to drop to the level below, didn't notice.

A flock of what seemed like *hundreds* of birds burst into the library. They went straight for the Ambassador, pecking at the top of his head, pulling at his robe, a miniature whirlwind of wings and beaks and claws.

He ducked, trying to protect himself, but he kept his hold on the stone.

'He's not going to let go,' Kalban said.

'We'll see about that.'

Meenakshi darted from behind the bookcase. The birds ignored her and focused their attacks on the Ambassador.

He was clutching the Fire of the East, but it was large enough for her to get her hands on it.

And put every bit of magic she could call up into it.

She thought Kalban said something, but she couldn't be certain over the sudden thundering in her ears.

'Meenakshi!' Chitralekha called, probably using her magic to make herself heard. 'I hope you know what you're doing, or Gopali's going to *kill* me.'

Magic was pouring out of the stone, almost too much to control. Perhaps it *would* have been too much to control for any *other* purpose, but Meenakshi didn't want to do anything requiring a high degree of precision. She fed the magic back into the Fire of the East as it came out. And it came out again, even stronger.

The stone grew warmer.

'What are you *doing*?' said the Yaunic Ambassador, still not letting go, although he looked terrified. 'You're going to kill us.'

'Meenakshi!' Kalban shouted, closer now. 'You're going to bring the building down on us.'

Meenakshi ignored them both.

The Fire of the East was practically a *real* fire now, blazing with light and heat—

The Yaunic Ambassador released it and backed away, but he'd forgotten about the hole in the floor. He fell through.

Something *else* was burning, something that had no physical form—

Meenakshi dropped the stone, unable to hold it any longer. It hit the floor with a crash like thunder.

All the magic filling the room stopped at once, leaving a void.

The stone, a fire agate and nothing more, cracked in two.

Meenakshi stared at it, breathing hard.

'Let me see!'

Kalban, appearing unexpectedly in front of Meenakshi, took her hands and turned them over. Meenakshi looked with some surprise at her blistered palms. That would be inconvenient but, at least, it was only temporary.

Kalban evidently came to the same conclusion, because he released her hands, shrugged, and said, 'You'd better postpone your Licence Tests by a couple of weeks.'

Meenakshi waited. She doubted she was getting off that lightly.

Sure enough, after a few more seconds to recover from the shock, Kalban burst out, 'Do you have any idea how *incredibly* stupid that was? You could have been killed—and you could have killed the Ambassador, though I grant that that wouldn't have been *entirely* a tragedy. You could have blown up this building—you could have caused *endless* trouble—'

'But she didn't,' said Chitralekha. 'And there's an alive but dazed Yaunic Ambassador that we'd better transport back to Rajgir.'

EPILOGUE

Meenakshi had managed to find herself a seat behind a pillar at the wedding reception. Evidently her uncle and Gopali were united in agreeing that destroying the Fire of the East entitled her to some leeway, because although they had both seen the book she had brought, neither had objected.

'Aren't you going to dance?' Chitralekha dropped into the chair next to her.

'Why would I dance?' Meenakshi peeked out from behind the pillar. Vasundhara was *very* flushed, though Meenakshi couldn't tell whether it was from wine or the general excitement. She was laughing more than usual. 'This is better.'

'*Much* better,' said Kalban, pulling up a chair on the other side. 'Tell me if Rati looks this way. She's trying to make me dance with the elder daughter of the High Lord of Vraja.'

'Don't you want to?'

'She's brought a *crocodile* with her.'

Meenakshi peered around the pillar again. 'She *has* brought a crocodile! And nobody would let me bring the griffon. The griffon doesn't even eat people.'

'So far, neither has the crocodile eaten anyone. I just want to make sure that *I'm* not the person who has to evade being eaten.'

Chitralekha laughed.

'Rambha's enjoying herself,' Kalban noted. 'She was more reasonable than I expected about everything.'

'She got the Sprite back *and* the perpetrators were caught,' said Chitralekha. 'She was angrier with Ravi than with Nalini. She still is. She thinks that at least after he was kidnapped, he should have realized what a bad idea it was and broken things off with Vasundhara.'

'Vasundhara wasn't going to stand for that.' Meenakshi shrugged. 'We'll have to be prepared for the possibility that someone will kidnap him again . . . or at least *she* will have to be prepared. She told me she's going to ask the Chair of Summoning if there's a way to make it difficult.'

'Asamanjas said you're taking your Licence Tests as soon as you go back,' Kalban said.

'Rambha didn't want me to postpone them. She said she doesn't want anyone using *that* excuse again, especially with Ravi a permanent fixture in Rajgir.' Meenakshi smiled suddenly. 'It's not just me. Everyone at the Royal Academy who's even halfway ready has to have a go at them this year. Clever Raman's having to take his earlier than he intended. The Master of the Academy says he's not happy about that at *all*. I wouldn't want to be Ravi if Clever Raman meets him down a dark alley.'

'Oh well. Ravi knew what he was letting himself in for when he decided to involve himself with a mortal.'

'You sound like Rambha.'

'What are you going to do after you've got your Licence?' Chitralekha asked curiously. 'Fellowship studies?'

'Oh, yes,' Meenakshi said. 'But not right away. I'm going to take a few months off and go to the Eastern Isles. Mother says she's found a place where it seems like the barrier between the Realms is thinning. It's having very interesting effects on magic, she says. We're going to study it.'

She didn't see the glance Kalban and Chitralekha exchanged.

'I'll speak to Rambha,' said Chitralekha. 'I'm sure she'll see reason. We can postpone all the Licence Tests by a few weeks, a month or two, maybe even a year. We wouldn't want to inconvenience Clever Raman.'

'Good luck,' said Kalban.

As a child, Aditi greatly enjoyed sports and once outswam a porpoise. She later had a chequered career that included working as a pet-food taster. In her downtime, she enjoys long-distance running and partying with her friends on Friday nights.

Just kidding. It's all fiction, just like the rest of this book.

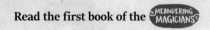

The Magicians of Madh

Something strange is afoot at the Royal Academy of Science, Magic and the Arts.

A standing statue sits down with a meditative smile . . .

A demigod is caught smuggling the Nectar of Immortality into the Mortal Realm . . .

Traders in Madh find their goods have been turned into djinn gold . . .

An illegal portal into the Inter-Realm has opened and no one knows who has done it . . .

A strange creature has been sighted in the vaults under the Academy . . .

Will Meenakshi and Kalban be able to get to the bottom of it all before the creature in the vault gets too powerful to control? Or is this a cover for something much more sinister—something that will destroy the city of Madh?

Read Book II of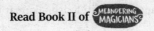

Murder in Melucha

Something strange is afoot at the Lotus Palace.

A guest is murdered after a boring state banquet . . .

A secret room full of scorpions is found . . .

A cloaked stranger passes on information . . .

Every marble statue seems to hold a secret . . .

In Melucha, children's alphabet books teach that H is for hemlock, so it is no particular surprise when someone is found murdered. But in a city where everyone has devious and twisted motives, and dire plans, it is not easy for Meenakshi and Kalban to find the murderer.

Read more by Aditi Krishnakumar in the

Songs of Freedom **series**

That Year at Manikoil

Madras, 1944

While World War II rages in Europe and the Japanese army draws closer to India, Raji and her sisters are sent off with their mother to stay in Manikoil, her mother's family village. But with her brother now a soldier in the British Indian Army and refugees fleeing from Malaya, Burma and other eastern countries back to India, Manikoil is no longer the peaceful haven it once was.

And while there is hope of Independence in the air, Raji is uncertain whether it will come to pass—and what it will truly mean for her and her family.

The Songs of Freedom series explores the lives of children across India during the struggle for independence.